"Where are you from?" Hunter asked.

"Me?" Chrissy squeaked. "Er . . . um, different places." *Anywhere but Iowa*, she thought.

"Is your dad in the military?" Hunter asked. Chrissy nodded. "What rank?" Hunter demanded.

"Oh, well, he's . . ." She couldn't think of any military ranks.

"I'll bet he's a general and you're too modest to say so."

"Something like that," Chrissy mumbled. This conversation was totally out of control.

"Is he stationed in San Francisco now?"

Chrissy could feel the trap closing around her. "Oh, no, I'm staying here with my cousin, Caroline."

"While your parents are abroad, I guess. I'll bet you go to Europe all the time. No wonder you're so creative. Art in Europe is way ahead of art here."

Stop this stupid charade right now, Chrissy told herself. *Let him know you're just an Iowa farm girl.*

Just then Hunter leaned forward and rested his warm hand on her arm. "Hey, Chrissy, would you like to come with me to a party tonight."

No! Chrissy's conscience said. *Tell him you're just a big phony. This can't go on!* Chrissy opened her mouth to speak. "Sure," she heard herself say. "I'd love to come, thank you."

Other books in the **SUGAR & SPICE** series:

Janet Quin-Harkin's

Sugar & Spice

Trading Places

IVY BOOKS • NEW YORK

Ivy Books
Published by Ballantine Books

Copyright © 1987 by Butterfield Press, Inc. & Janet Quin-Harkin

Produced by Butterfield Press, Inc.
133 Fifth Avenue
New York, New York 10003

Library of Congress Catalog Card Number: 86-91847

ISBN 0-8041-0027-6

Manufactured in the United States of America

First Edition: June 1987

TRADING PLACES

Janet Quin-Harkin

Chapter 1

Chrissy Madden sat on the broad window seat and stared out into the soft, velvet night. It had been one of those hot Indian summer days that sometimes take San Francisco by surprise in October. Now the night air wafted in through the open window, still warm and scented with the smells of the city. The fragrance of the salty water from the bay below, the roasted coffee from the Italian café nearby, and the diesel fumes from the buses making the steep climb to Nob Hill became familiar to Chrissy. She had also become accustomed to the unique sounds of the city—the same sounds that kept her awake during her first nights in San Francisco. The cable car bell clanging incessantly as it passed each cross street, car horns and emergency sirens, tugboat hoots, clattering footsteps and loud voices of the people on the sidewalks, and the distant foghorns of the Golden Gate Bridge all were part of a symphony so different from the sounds on the farm back home in Iowa.

A gentle breeze fluttered the pages of Chrissy's writing tablet on the window ledge. She grabbed the paper before a playful wind could sweep it away. She had written an entire page already, but felt as if she'd barely started—there was so much to say.

My dear, darling Mom, Dad, Bonnie, and the cats (I suppose I should include my brothers, but I want them to know they are not dear and darling —they are in the doghouse because they haven't written me one single letter in the two months I've been gone! Three lines scribbled on the bottom of one of Mom's letters does not count, Will Madden!!!) . . .

She paused and smiled as she imagined her brother Will's reaction when her mother read the letter out loud. She sat by the window thinking, sensing the emptiness of the apartment behind her, then picked up her pen again:

I'm having a good time here, but I do miss all of you—even the boys, if you can believe it! Aunt Edith's house is so quiet and orderly. It's not even a house, exactly. It's really the third-floor apartment in a huge house way up on the top of a hill. Anyway, here nobody ever yells or gets excited. Can you imagine our house being quiet and orderly like that? No way! You don't know how much I long for a good, old-fashioned fight with all of us yelling, each trying to be louder than everybody else, and even Bonnie going wild and dancing around barking. I even miss your teasing, believe it or not. Caroline never teases. She is very nice to me and we get along well. Sometimes we even seem more like sisters instead of long-lost cousins.

Apart from the politeness and the quiet, I reckon I'm surviving pretty well in the city. It took a while, but I feel pretty confident that I can handle school now. Maxwell must be at least ten times bigger than Danbury High. For the first couple of weeks I was terrified that I wouldn't be able to keep up with the classes. But now I know that I'm just as smart as most of the kids here—even smarter than some of them. I've also found out that I know some things they don't know, which is a good feeling, so it all equals out.

The kids at school have completely accepted me into their group now. In fact, if Ben were here, everything would be just perfect. I still miss him so much. How is he? Does he still stop by for your cornbread? Is he lonely without me? On evenings like this, when I'm all alone in the apartment, I think of him a lot. Caroline has gone to a concert with her parents. I was invited, too, but I have the usual ton of homework, and besides, I really don't like modern music too much. We went to a flute concerto last week, but it sounded more like a cat fight to me.

Chrissy paused again and tore off a second sheet. Glancing over at the clock on the dresser, she saw that it was nearly ten o'clock. *I wonder what everyone is doing at home?* she thought. Out the window the lights of a cable car inch down the hill like a giant lightning bug. Chrissy gazed down toward the wharf, where she noticed a cruise ship strung with colored lights like a Christmas tree. She sighed contentedly—there was always something happening in San Francisco.

Chrissy continued writing:

I'm really glad I decided to come here. You were right, Mom (as usual!). I'm getting quite an education here, and I don't just mean school. San Francisco is a completely different world from Danbury! It has taken some getting used to, but I really feel at home in the city now. I bet you'd hardly recognize me. I'm so cool about crossing streets and behaving like a sophisticated city person.

Chrissy reached for the finished pages of her letter as another gust swept in through the open window. But the wind lifted the pages off the window ledge, and before she could catch them, they fluttered out into the darkness of the street below.

"Oh, Jeepers!" Chrissy cried, leaping up and peering out. In the patches of light shining from the windows of the apartments below, she thought she spotted her letter partially hidden in a bush.

She hesitated for a moment, staring out at the deserted street. Then, after carefully making sure the door of the apartment was unlocked, Chrissy sprinted down the two flights of stairs, past the front porch and around to the side of the house, where she retrieved the two sheets of paper from the bush. She was just returning to the porch when the wind whipped up again. This time it wasn't a gentle breeze but a fierce gale straight from the ocean. Chrissy ran for the house, but she wasn't quick enough. The building's front door slammed shut in her face, leaving her shivering on the porch outside.

She tried the door, but it was firmly locked. "Holy mazoley," she sighed, bringing her hands up to her face in an elaborate gesture. Another gust of wind blew up from the wharf, and Chrissy felt her skin prickle with goose bumps. She was dressed only in her pink baby-doll pajamas, and nobody was home in the apartment to let her back in.

Chrissy stared at the row of door bells, wondering if she dare disturb any of the neighbors. She had met a few of them on the stairs and on the porch, but was embarrassed to be seen in her pajamas.

I could always sit on the porch until the others get home, she thought. *The concert will be over pretty soon.* But then she reconsidered. Caroline's family went to a reception after the concert. *Do I wait around on the porch until after midnight?* she asked herself.

Now she recalled what she'd written in her letter — that she was comfortable living in the city — but was now reminded that the city was not a safe place. She'd heard a lot of scary stories, and her aunt and uncle were always telling her to be careful. Chrissy decided she'd better not hang around on the porch alone at night — especially not in her pajamas.

Then she noticed the bougainvillea. The huge vine climbed over one side of the porch and made its way up the side of the house.

Should I? Chrissy thought to herself. She certainly

didn't doubt her climbing ability. Her brother had once dared her to climb through her bedroom window back home at the farm by way of the big old cottonwood tree. She'd had to walk along a limb of the tree, then reach across to her window. That seemed much scarier than climbing up this creeper. But she hesitated to climb the side of an apartment house in the middle of a big city. *What if someone sees me?* she wondered.

The wind was blowing in earnest now—a cold wind straight from the Alaskan current out in the Pacific. Chrissy's teeth began to chatter.

That settles it, she decided. *I'm not going to stand around freezing for the next two hours.*

She glanced up and down the street. For once there was nobody in sight on the sidewalk, and the cars sped past too quickly to see her. Chrissy swung herself onto the creeper and began to climb.

The trunk was huge, and twisted into convenient footholds at the bottom. When Chrissy reached the top of the porch, she paused to catch her breath and look around. Above her she could see her own window, wide open and within easy reach. The only obstacle was the window on the floor below hers. It was also open, and the light on. Chrissy tried to remember who lived in the second-floor apartment, but she didn't think she'd ever met her downstairs neighbors.

"With any luck," she told herself as she inched upward again, "nobody will even notice that I'm—"

At that moment the piece of vine she was reaching for tore loose from the wall. Chrissy yelled in surprise as she swung away from the house, then whipped forward. She put a hand out and grabbed a firmer branch. Her heart pounded so loudly, she was sure that the sound echoed back from the house next door. Then she looked up into a face peering down from the second-floor window, only a few inches above her. Both she and the face screamed at the same time, then the window slammed shut and the face disappeared.

Chrissy clung to the vine, not knowing what to do next. If she climbed any higher, she would have to pass the second-floor window, and she didn't want to risk that. She considered lowering herself to the ground, but getting down didn't look as easy as getting up. She waited for the face to reappear in the window, so she could have a chance to explain—maybe the face would even invite her inside—but nothing moved behind the glass panes.

Then Chrissy heard a car screech to a stop in front of the house. She looked down and saw a policeman get out of the car before she could move. She was temporarily blinded by a brilliant light.

"Stay where you are. Don't move!" commanded a voice in the darkness below her.

Stupid thing to say, Chrissy thought. *Where am I going to go?* So she remained, clinging with hands and feet that were becoming colder and stiffer every moment. At last someone opened the window above her head. Chrissy looked up, expecting to find a helping hand. Instead she found herself looking at a gun.

"Okay. Come on up quietly," the policeman instructed. "I don't want any trouble."

"But you don't understand, I'm not doing anything wrong. I live here—in the apartment above this one." As always when Chrissy was scared, the words came out in an almost incomprehensible torrent. "You see, I was in the middle of writing to my folks, only it was so warm that I was sitting by the open window. I'd finished two pages when there was this enormous gust of wind that blew them away, so I ran downstairs, but then the wind blew the front door shut and I got locked out by mistake. I was only trying to climb back into my room."

The wind snatched at Chrissy's hair and at her pajamas, cutting right through the thin cotton. "Look, Officer, I don't think I can hang on much longer," Chrissy said, her teeth beginning to chatter again. "Could I please come inside?"

The policeman's stern expression softened. "I think I can put my gun away," he said, tucking it into his belt with a grin. "You don't look like a dangerous criminal to me, and besides, I can't imagine where you would conceal a weapon." He barked some words into a walkie-talkie then reached down and lifted her easily into the room. Chrissy stood blinking in the strong light, more conscious than ever of her flimsy pajamas under the amused gaze of the policeman.

"Now, let's get this straightened out," he said. "Would you come here a moment, Mrs. Langdon?"

Chrissy focused on the tall gray-haired woman cautiously entering the room. *I bet Mrs. Langdon would be a terrific witch for Halloween!* she thought.

"The girl says that she lives in this building on the next floor up," the policeman said.

"Nonsense," Mrs. Langdon replied, her voice quivering. "The Kirbys live on the third floor. They just have one daughter, and this is not her. No, they look

very similar, but she is definitely not the Kirby girl."
She sat down slowly on the blue velvet sofa. "Goodness, my heart still hasn't stopped palpitating. . . ."

"But I'm living with the Kirbys now," Chrissy explained. "My name's Chrissy Madden. I'm the Kirbys' niece."

"So where are these Kirbys?" the officer asked.

"They're not here right now. They went to a concert. I could have gone, too, but I don't like modern music. They should be back any minute, and then they can tell you," Chrissy said hopefully.

"You say you don't recognize this young lady?" the policeman asked the woman.

Mrs. Langdon peered at Chrissy over her glasses, frowned and looked away again. "I said I didn't the first time. I rarely make mistakes, Officer."

"But you must have seen me," Chrissy said. "I've been here for about two months now. I go up and down the stairs all the time."

"I rarely go out," Mrs. Langdon said. "I have only seen one girl come from the floor upstairs, and that is the Kirbys' daughter."

Chrissy looked around her in disbelief. What had started as a simple letter home had turned into a nightmare. She wondered if the officer would take her down to police headquarters. What would happen if the police remembered that she had stolen a bulldozer the month before to help save the park? This time they probably wouldn't let her off so easily.

"I want her arrested for breaking and entering," Mrs. Langdon was saying. "She was obviously attempting to burglarize my apartment."

"Would I be dressed like this if I were a burglar?" Chrissy asked in amazement.

"This city if full of strange people," Mrs. Langdon said coldly. "Nothing would surprise me about the way people dress here. I might have been murdered in my bed, Officer. I want her arrested!"

"I think maybe you'd better come down to headquarters, miss," the policeman said to Chrissy. "Until we can get your uncle or aunt to identify you."

Chrissy looked around desperately, and a small ray of hope dawned in her brain, Mrs. Langdon's constant complaining reminded her of the previous evening.

"Your apartment must be right below my bedroom," she said to Mrs. Langdon. "You were the one who thumped on the floor last night when I was doing my aerobics!"

Mrs. Langdon turned to stare at Chrissy with frosty blue eyes. "That was you? I might have known—the Kirbys' daughter has always been a well-behaved little thing. Goodness, my entire ceiling shook! The chandelier was swaying. I thought it was an earthquake, young lady. I was only lucky the plaster didn't crack and fall on my head. Next time I suggest you do your—your—:

Chrissy gave an embarrassed grin. "Aerobics," she said.

"Well, just don't make such a racket next time."

"So you do know this girl?" the officer interrupted.

"I know about my ceiling nearly falling on my head last night," Mrs. Langdon answered.

"That proves I live upstairs, doesn't it?" Chrissy asked the policeman hopefully.

He grinned. "Sounds like it."

"Thanks, Officer," Chrissy said in relief. "In fact, I just remembered that I left the door to the apartment unlocked. You see, I thought I'd only be gone for a minute. I guess I should have taken more care with the outside door. Anyway, I can show you a picture of me with Caroline and my Aunt Edith and Uncle Richard —for extra proof."

"Okay. Let's go," the policeman said, grinning.

"You're not going to arrest her or anything?" Mrs. Langdon demanded.

The policeman shrugged his shoulders. "I don't think she's done anything wrong—except maybe damage the creeper outside."

"What about scaring me half to death?" Mrs. Langdon called as the policeman shepherded Chrissy toward the door.

"Sorry, Mrs. Langdon, but I'm not going to arrest her," the officer replied. "Have a good night now."

With the policeman now on her side, Chrissy was fast returning to her usual mischievous self. "Good night, Mrs. Langdon," she called. "It was nice meeting you." Then she bounded up the stairs next to the policeman.

She was half asleep, feeling relaxed and secure again, when she heard Caroline tiptoe into the room.

"Are you still awake, Chrissy?" Caroline whispered. Chrissy peeked out from under the covers. "You should have come to the concert," Caroline said as she hung up her jacket. "It was really exciting. There was this crazy man and he started shouting that the conductor had stolen his concerto. They had to get the security guards to take him away. Anything exciting happen here?"

Chrissy opened her mouth and then shut it again. "Exciting?" she asked, trying to keep from laughing. "No, nothing really exciting happened. I just wrote a letter home, that's about all. A very ordinary evening, in fact."

"I hope you weren't too bored on your own," Caroline went on, sinking onto her bed and taking off a shoe.

Chrissy turned over with a big yawn. "I survived okay," she said, grinning to herself as she pulled her covers up over her head.

Chapter 2

"Mom! Mom, are you home? Guess what!" Chrissy heard her cousin yell down the front hall.

Chrissy and Aunt Edith sat together in the kitchen, drinking a late afternoon cup of peppermint tea. They looked at each other in surprise at the outburst from down the hall.

"Is that Caroline?" Aunt Edith asked, giving Chrissy an amused look.

"Sounds more like me," Chrissy commented with a grin as the front door slammed loudly.

"Mom, where are you?" Chrissy could hear Caroline's voice approaching. Two seconds later Caroline burst into the kitchen, her face glowing. "Oh, there you are. Hi, Chrissy. Is there any tea left? I'm so thirsty. I ran all the way home," she panted, the words tumbling out as she picked up the Chinese teapot and took down a handmade ceramic mug from the rack. "You'll never guess what happened," she went on as she poured tea into the mug. "I am so excited!"

Chrissy looked at her cousin with interest. During the two months she'd lived with Caroline's family, she had never seen Caroline as enthusiastic as she was now. Caroline never yelled or slammed doors or jumped up and down. Chrissy had thought she was the only person in sophisticated San Francisco who did things like that. Was a little of her own personality beginning to rub off on her cousin? she wondered.

Wouldn't it be funny if Caroline became loud and crazy like me by the time I leave next year? she thought with a grin. *And what if I became like her? I've been trying to act more sophisticated around school, but if I go home acting all ladylike, and not yelling or running around anymore, my family won't believe it's me!* Then Chrissy's thoughts turned serious: *Do I really want to be like Caroline? I admire the way she's so cool and elegant, but she takes life so seriously most of the time!*

"Okay, spill the beans," Chrissy said, looking at her cousin in anticipation. "You got a perfect score on your history test?"

"Better than that," Caroline said, sitting down opposite her and taking a gulp of the steaming tea.

"Baryshnikov asked you to dance with him?" Chrissy guessed, now even more curious to know what could possibly have caused Caroline to get so excited.

"I wish," Caroline said, looking up with a big smile. "But almost as good. You know the art fair they have at our school, Mom?"

"You mean the big art exhibition for all the high

schools? You took me to it last year, remember?" Aunt Edith said.

Caroline nodded. "Well, this year they've asked me to be on the committee," she announced grandly, her eyes wide with pleasure.

Chrissy continued to stare at her cousin. She knew that she and Caroline often had different priorities, but an art fair really seemed a weird thing to get excited about. *That proves it—I'm certainly not turning into another Caroline yet*, she decided. *What's the big deal about being on the committee for an art fair? It would be different if one of the judges was Tom Cruise or Bruce Springsteen!*

"I'm really happy for you, darling," Aunt Edith said. "That's wonderful."

"Yeah, that's great," Chrissy echoed. She knew Caroline expected her to be excited too.

But Caroline must have caught a glimpse of her cousin's face, because she put down her mug and explained, "It's a huge art fair, Chrissy. Our school hosts it every year for students from schools all around San Francisco. It's a big honor to be on the planning committee. And it's not just the fair itself. The committee also gets to plan all the social events. There's a formal reception to open it, and lots of important people from the art world come. Then there's a super dance at the end of it, so it's a lot of responsibility."

Caroline took another sip of tea and looked at her mother. "They've only asked one junior besides me, Mom. All the rest are seniors—they're all the sort of people you would expect to be asked, creative and popular too. I don't know why they ever thought of me."

"I think you're a natural for the committee, Cara," Chrissy said encouragingly. "Everyone at school likes you, and you do terrific art work. Look at these mugs you made!"

Caroline flushed. "Yes, but you should see some of the really good stuff people do. Mine are just amateur."

"Don't put yourself down, Caroline," her mother said firmly. "You show a lot of talent, both in organizing and in art. I think your work is very promising."

"You're prejudiced," Caroline suggested.

"Maybe," Aunt Edith agreed. "But don't forget, you are my daughter, so I expect it runs in the family."

She laughed to show she was only joking, but Caroline nodded seriously.

"That might have been one of the reasons they asked me," she admitted. "Mr. Yamagata wants to know if you'll be a judge this year, Mom."

Now Mrs. Kirby beamed the same way Caroline had when she'd first burst into the kitchen with her news. "Well, I'm flattered," she said. "Tell them I'd be delighted, Caroline."

"That's great, Mom," Caroline said. "I know you'll be a terrific judge. It will be so much fun—something you and I can do together. I'll be a hostess at the reception and you'll be one of the distinguished guests."

"I hope you'll find enough time for it," Aunt Edith said thoughtfully. "You know how hard it's been for you to fit in your ballet and your homework as it is."

"I'll make time, Mom," Caroline said firmly. "Besides, we'll have most of our meetings during the study period and lunch hour."

"Just as long as you don't get too tired," Caroline's

mother said, looking at her daughter with concern. "You can only push yourself so far, you know."

"I'll survive, I'm tough like you," Caroline replied. Finishing her tea, she jumped up again. "I really want to do this, Mom. It means I've arrived at school, that I'm the sort of person other people have finally noticed. I'm not a nobody any more."

"You never were a nobody," her mother said with a smile. "I've always thought you were very special."

Caroline walked over to her mother and wrapped her arms around her mother's shoulders. "As I said before, you are totally prejudiced," she said softly. "You should try having four kids, like Chrissy's mom, then you wouldn't think your one and only was so wonderful all the time!"

"Of course I would," her mother said, patting Caroline's arm. "I would think all four of you were wonderful, the way Aunt Ingrid thinks of Chrissy and the boys."

As Chrissy watched Aunt Edith and Caroline bending close together, she couldn't help but feel homesick. Her own mother was so far away, and Chrissy hadn't had a real hug in two whole months. She got up, her chair squeaking on the tiled kitchen floor. "I'd better finish my homework," she said quietly, "or I'll never get that essay finished."

Aunt Edith looked up and glanced at the clock on the wall. "Heavens, is that the time?" she exclaimed. "I'd better get back to the gallery. We have a reception for that new painter tonight. You know the one I told you about—Milo. He paints only in natural dyes. He squeezes some spinach and beetroot on a canvas, and voilà! Milo certainly gets some interesting results!"

She stood up and reached for her purse. "See you girls later," she said. "Don't wait dinner for me. You can finish off that quiche in the fridge."

As the door shut behind her, Chrissy began to gather the teacups and carry them over to the sink.

"I'd better get myself organized," Caroline went on brightly. "If I'm going to have all this extra stuff to do, I'll have to budget my time very carefully. Maybe I'll ask Alex to make me out a timetable—he's good at stuff like that. How long do you think it takes me to eat breakfast? Do you think I can squeeze in an hour of homework before school? I hope my teachers accept my papers with cornflakes on them!"

She paused and walked over to the sink, where Chrissy was now washing up. "You're very quiet," she said. "Is something wrong?"

"Wrong?" Chrissy asked, not looking up from the sink. "No, nothing's wrong. I just feel like being quiet."

"That's highly suspicious for you," Caroline said. "Are you feeling okay?"

"I told you, I feel fine," Chrissy said. "I just didn't have anything to say. I don't know anything about art fairs."

"Chrissy?" Caroline asked hesitantly. "Are you upset about the art fair? I can't understand why that would bother you. You've never seemed interested in art before. I'd have thought you'd feel happy for me."

Chrissy finished drying the last mug and hung it back on the rack. "Of course I'm happy for you, Cara," she said. "I've never seen you so excited. It's just that I was thinking I had life pretty much under control here, and now I can't help feeling like an outsider again. If I'd stayed at home, I'd have been a somebody this year too. I'd have been head cheerleader and on the student council and the prom committee. All the freshmen would point to me and whisper, 'Wow, that's Chrissy Madden.'"

Caroline nodded with understanding. "You'll still have your senior year in Danbury, Chrissy," she said. "And all the freshmen will point to you and whisper, 'Wow, that's Chrissy Madden. She went to school in California!'"

Chrissy managed a smile. "You're right," she said. "I'm sorry if I was acting like an old grouch."

"That's okay. You know, Chrissy, you've made lots of friends already this year," Caroline went on enthusiastically. "All my friends are your friends now. You'll probably have so much to do, you won't even miss me if I'm not around much."

"I guess you're right," Chrissy said. "I really do like all your friends, and there's so much in San Francisco that I haven't done yet. Don't wory about me—you go and organize your fantastic art fair. I'll be just fine!"

"I'm going to phone Alex right now," Caroline said, already halfway to the kitchen door. "I want to see if he can do that timetable for me tonight. I am going to make time for this art fair, or end up a squeezed spinach on one of Milo's canvases!" She looked back at Chrissy and gave her a huge grin as she disappeared down the hall.

Chrissy stood beside the sink, looking after her cousin. *Of course I don't mind that Caroline's going to be* on an important committee, she told herself. *In fact, I'm really happy for her. I've never seen her so excited. It's great for her. And I've got to keep up my grades and write lots of letters home, so I've got plenty to keep me busy. I probably won't even notice if she doesn't have time for me anymore.*

Chapter 3

Chrissy sat alone on a bench in the little park she and
Caroline had fought so hard to save. It was a sweet
victory to eat lunch in that park every day, knowing that
their efforts had stopped a big developer from turning it
into a parking garage. Chrissy especially enjoyed eating
there. Back in Danbury she had walked down the dusty
path from the high school to her grandmother's house for
lunch every day. Her younger brothers joined her from
the elementary school, and her grandmother always had
a huge lunch ready—thick soup in winter with home-
made meat pies, or cold salads with fresh fruits and
vegetables when the weather got warmer. From her
grandmother's kitchen window she could look out across
acres of corn and smell the sweet, fresh scent of cut hay
and roses. During her first days at Maxwell High she
felt trapped by the gray walls of the school courtyard.
This park had been just what she needed to escape from

the noise and bustle of a huge high school and get her head in order again.

In fact, lunch hour had become Chrissy's favorite time of day. All of Caroline's friends usually assembled in the park, sitting under the big magnolia tree on hot days and beneath the shelter of the building next door on foggy ones, talking and laughing, trading food and good-natured insults. Chrissy put her sandwich down on top of the brown paper bag. Somehow, a turkey sandwich with only two slices of turkey and lots of alfalfa sprouts wasn't very appealing when compared to her grandmother's midday feasts. But she had promised her mother that she would fit in with her California relatives, so she ate the sprouts while recalling vegetable soup and beef pies.

Several sparrows hopped around her feet, looking up at her hopefully. Chrissy tore off a piece of crust and tossed it down to them. They fought over the bread, cheeping excitedly. Chrissy smiled at them fondly and threw down another piece. Without warning there was a swoop of wings, and an enormous, snowy white sea gull glided in to scatter the sparrows and claim the bread for itself.

"Shoo," Chrissy said, looking at the enormous bird with distrust. "That was for the sparrows, not you."

The sea gull gave her a withering stare from his beady eyes and hopped up onto the side of her bench.

"Shoo," Chrissy said again, uneasily. The bird looked very large and very fierce close up. Chrissy moved down the bench. Three more sea gulls glided in silently to join the first one. They stood around her in a circle, staring at her. Feeling even more uneasy, Chrissy got to her feet.

"Shoo, go away," she said, waving her arms. The sea gulls moved back a few inches, but continued to stare. Chrissy thought of a movie she had seen on TV —Alfred Hitchcock's *The Birds*. The movie had been scary enough, but now it was happening for real!

"I think I've had enough lunch now," she said to herself calmly. "I'll just get my lunch bag and go back to school."

As she moved to pick up her sandwich, the biggest sea gull swooped over and grabbed it. The large beak so close to her hand was too much for Chrissy. She clutched her school bag and ran across the park.

She was passing the magnolia tree when she bumped into Alex.

"Hey, what's the big hurry?" he asked, holding her arms gently to steady her. "Lunch isn't over for another ten minutes." He looked at her face. "Is something wrong, Chrissy?"

"Those sea gulls stole my lunch," she said in a small voice.

"Sea gulls?"

"Yes, sea gulls. I got scared."

Chrissy noticed Alex trying to suppress a grin. "Scared of the sea gulls?" he asked.

"It's not funny, Alex. They came and stood all around me," Chrissy said, "and one of them took my sandwich. They're really big, and I didn't like the way they looked at me out of those nasty little eyes."

Alex laughed. "But Chrissy, sea gulls can't hurt you. You just have to shoo them away."

"I said shoo," Chrissy answered, "and they wouldn't go."

"You are funny," Alex said warmly. He slipped his arm around Chrissy's shoulder. "Do you want me to try to save that sandwich for you?"

"It's too late now," Chrissy said. "And besides, I'm not that wild about alfalfa!"

"I'll walk you back to school then," Alex said. "I came up here expecting to find the rest of the gang. Were you all alone?"

"That's right," Chrissy said. "All alone with the sea gulls."

"So where is everybody?"

"Everybody seems to have something to do except me," Chrissy replied. "Caroline is at another committee meeting, and all the others seem to be busy with clubs or newspapers or sports."

"Poor old Chrissy," Alex said. "You sound really down."

"I am feeling a bit down," Chrissy confessed. "Just when I thought I really fitted in here, everyone disappears in opposite directions. They've all got important things to do, and I just feel like a tag-along again."

"Of course you fit in here," Alex said kindly. "Everyone likes you, Chrissy. It's just that lots of things are happening all at once—Caroline's got the art fair, Maria's got student government, Justine's got field hockey, and I've got soccer. What about Tracy and George? Are they busy?"

"Chess club," Chrissy said, making a face. "They play chess every day at lunch."

"You could go along with them if you wanted," Alex suggested.

Chrissy made a face. "I don't think I can sit still long enough for a game of chess."

Alex grinned. "It was just a thought."

"Let's face it, Alex," Chrissy said. "Out of all the activities here at Maxwell, I'm not much good at any of them."

"But you can do lots of things," Alex said. "Look how well you organized Caroline's surprise party last month. I bet any committee would be glad to have you on it, Chrissy. What would you really like to do?"

"Oh, I don't know," Chrissy said hesitantly. "Don't worry about me. I'll be fine. I don't want anyone to feel I'm in the way here."

"You're not in the way," Alex said. "I like having you around. If I could disguise you as a guy, I'd take you to soccer practice with me."

Chrissy laughed. "You're so nice, Alex. Caroline's lucky to have you."

"That's me—Mr. Wonderful," Alex said kiddingly, but Chrissy could tell he was flattered.

As they walked down the hill in silence, Chrissy stole a sideways glance at him. *He is so nice*, she thought. *If he didn't belong to Caroline, I think I could fall for him.* Chrissy still hadn't forgotten Caroline's recent suspicions about Alex and herself, and she understood how Caroline wouldn't want to lose a guy like Alex.

I would never do that to Caroline anyway, or to Ben either, she thought. *It's so hard having a boyfriend a thousand miles away. I guess I just miss having a special guy of my own around all the time. I miss walking along, holding hands and having him sit close beside me and put his arm around me. I miss those heart-to-heart talks. But most of all I miss that special look that makes me feel on top of the world.*

"I told Caroline I'd meet her by the steps and walk to Chemistry class with her," Alex said, interrupting Chrissy's thoughts. "She's so busy now I have to make an appointment to see her."

"I guess it's even worse since this art fair came up," Chrissy commented. "We never get to see her at home. She's either at ballet or the art fair committee or she's doing homework."

Alex nodded. "Sometimes I wish she'd slow down and not push herself so hard, but she's been really excited about the art fair."

"I'll say," Chrissy agreed. "I'd no idea Caroline could get excited. She was always so cool before, and now suddenly she's been rushing around and yelling—she's sounding more like me every day."

Alex turned and smiled at her. "And are you becoming poised and sophisticated?" he asked.

"Holy cow, no way," Chrissy replied with a big grin.

"That's good," Alex said.

They turned the corner and his expression changed. "There she is now," he said.

It's a good thing I'm not falling for him, Chrissy decided, looking at Alex's face. *It's pretty obvious who he cares about.*

"Hi, Cara!" he called.

Caroline ran down the steps toward him. "Hi, Alex," she said. As he took her into his arms and spun her around, Chrissy felt a stab of jealousy. "Put me down, you crazy idiot," Caroline said with a giggle. "People are watching."

"Let them watch," Alex said, lowering her to the ground.

"I don't know about you, Alex," Caroline said. She smoothed her hair back into place, revealing cheeks still pink with embarrassment. "Have you been up to the park for lunch?"

"I was going," he said. "But I met Chrissy on her way back, being chased by hundreds of sea gulls."

"Alex," Chrissy said, feeling like a fool as Caroline looked at her curiously. "A sea gull took my lunch, and I guess I got a bit scared."

"I don't blame you," Caroline said. "Those birds are such pests sometimes. Alex, do you remember that one that snatched Justine's hot dog right off the bun?" She turned back to Chrissy. "Weren't the others up at the park?"

"They all had something to do, except me," Chrissy said, then realized that it sounded as if she were complaining. She didn't want her cousin to think she was unhappy in California, so she asked quickly, "How was your meeting today? Did you get a lot done?"

Caroline's face broke into a big smile. "We had such a fun time," she said, moving into place between Alex and Chrissy and linking her arms with theirs. "Those guys on the committee are so funny! We were planning the theme for the ball today. Sacha thought we should do 'Sunday in the Park with George,' like that French painting, and Dominic said he didn't want to stand like a statue all evening, then Rainbow said she's very into Gauguin right now and couldn't we do a South Seas thing? We all laughed about that, because none of the people in Gauguin's paintings wear clothes. Well, we didn't think that would be allowed. Anyway, I'm a little too modest to wear a mask and nothing else! Then Hunter suggested calling it 'Carnival in Venice' and flooding the gym to look like the Venice canals. We all thought that sounded terrific, so we're going to do it."

"Flood the gym?" Alex asked, astonished.

Caroline giggled. "Well, not really flood the gym, but have the carnival in Venice as our theme. Then we can wear those beautiful masks they have for the real carnival there. You know, butterflies and feathers and those beautiful Pierrot clowns!"

Chrissy looked from Alex to Caroline. Right now she felt exactly like a little hick again, fresh off the farm. She had no idea what Caroline was talking about, and got the impression that she was probably the only person at Maxwell High who hadn't been to the carnival in Venice. *And their names,* Chrissy thought, *Rainbow and Hunter and Sacha. How do people get names like that?*

"Sounds like a lot of fun," Alex said. "I can't wait to see it."

"It's going to be absolutely wonderful, Alex," Caroline said. "But we're going to need all the help we can get. I realy want everything to look good."

"How about Chrissy?" Alex suggested. "She was just saying she feels left out with everyone else rushing about here and there."

"Sure," Caroline said, smiling at Chrissy. "I thought you had plenty to keep you busy, but if you want, we'd love you to help with the decorations."

"What about now?" Alex asked. "Can't you use her on your committee somehow? You know how good she is at organizing things."

"Well, the trouble is—" Caroline began.

"It's okay, Alex," Chrissy cut in. "I understand about the committee. Caroline was especially chosen for it, and it's a big honor for her. There's no way she could take me along. Please don't worry about me. I'll be just fine as long as I stay away from those sea gulls."

She gave Caroline what she hoped was the convincing smile of a truly contented person. Caroline looked across at her cousin and then at Alex.

"We could use some help on Saturday if you're free, Chrissy," Caroline said. "We're going to get the gym ready then."

"The gym?" Alex asked. "For the dance, you mean?"

"No, for the exhibition," Caroline said.

"I thought it was always held outside, in the courtyard."

"It always was," Caroline said. "But remember it rained last year and the artwork nearly got ruined. We don't want to risk that again, so the principal said we could use the old gym if we clean it up first."

"Where's the old gym?" Chrissy asked.

"You probably haven't seen it," Caroline explained. "It's across the street, next to the football field. Inside there are these marble columns and things, so it's not much use as a gym. In fact, it will be a great place for an art show."

"Sounds terrific," Chrissy said. "I'd love to come help set it up, if you're sure I won't be in the way."

"Of course you won't," Caroline replied. "In fact, I'm sure you'll be a big help. The kids on the committee are great at coming up with ideas, but they're not too practical. I'd like you to meet everyone, Chrissy. They're so funny. We spend most of the time laughing."

"I can't wait," Chrissy said, pushing through the big double doors of the school with Caroline and Alex. "I've never met anyone called Rainbow or Hunter before. Are those names for real?"

"Sure they are," Caroline said. "Kids get called all sorts of weird things in San Francisco. I was almost a weirdo in kindergarten because my name was Caroline and not Strawberry or Cream."

"You wouldn't have made a good Strawberry or Cream," Alex said teasingly. "A Liver or Spinach maybe . . ."

"Alex Bauman, you are horrible," Caroline said, giving his arm a playful punch. "I don't know why I bother to hang around with you. I think I'll run off with one of the gorgeous guys on the committee instead. I bet Hunter thinks I look like a Strawberry."

Again Chrissy felt like an outsider, watching Caroline and Alex. Again she thought wistfully about having someone special to tease and just have fun with. *I remember how Ben and I used to tease each other*, she mused. *I could always win a fight by tickling him.*"

"Earth to Chrissy," Caroline said, touching her arm.

"Excuse me?" Chrissy asked. She'd been daydreaming. She and Ben were chasing each other around the haystack. She threatened to tickle him until he kissed her. Ben gave up right away and kissed her, but she tickled him anyway.

"Alex asked you if you'd like a ride home tonight since he's got the car," Caroline said. "I have to stay late, as usual, but there's no reason why you shouldn't get a ride."

"Oh, thanks," Chrissy said. "I'd like that, Alex."

"See you by the door after school, then," Alex said.

"Okay, see you later," Chrissy replied, turning off into the girls' bathroom.

As she pushed open the door she heard Alex's deep voice echoing down the tiled hall. "I'm really glad you got her involved with the art fair, Cara. She was feeling totally out of it, poor kid."

"I just hope getting her involved is the right thing." Caroline's voice faded into the distance. "I don't want her to feel more out of it around people she has noth-ing . . ."

Chrissy could no longer make out their words. She stood inside the bathroom door and stared at herself thoughtfully in the mirror. Then she took out her brush and ran it through her long blond hair.

Chapter 4

"Holy cow, what a dump!" Chrissy exclaimed when she and Caroline pushed open the big oak door and stood in the aquariumlike gloom of the old gym.

"Chrissy!" Caroline exclaimed. "This is a historic building. It was built near the turn of the century, when the classical style was in fashion for schools."

As Chrissy's eyes adjusted to the gloom, she absorbed the scene inside the gym. The green marble pillars lined up along each side of the room stood in a floor thick with dirt, and the sturdy wooden bleachers had piles of trash underneath. Early morning sunshine streamed through the grimy skylight, illuminating dancing dust particles. It reminded Chrissy of a scene out of a fairy tale, where the hero discovers a castle asleep under a spell. The gym looked as if it had been asleep for at least a hundred years.

"Wow, this place is weird, Cara," Chrissy said

softly. "What are all those pillar things there for? And all those statues up there?"

"They're to make it elegant."

"Who needs an elegant gym?" Chrissy asked. "How can you play a good game of basketball if you have to keep dodging these ridiculous things? Knowing me, I'd have a statue fall on my head within five minutes."

Caroline smiled. "Well, I guess they played more elegant games in those days." As Caroline spoke, Chrissy heard a great burst of eerie laughter echo through the room from behind the farthest pillar.

"Oh, some of the kids are already here," Caroline said. "Come on down and meet them."

"Okay," Chrissy replied, hesitating as she spotted the small group clustered around a pillar. She was glad they hadn't noticed yet that she and Caroline had arrived.

"Chrissy," Caroline whispered as they set off across the gym. "Don't say holy cow, okay?"

"I'll try not to," Chrissy replied, grinning broadly at Caroline's serious face. "You know what I'm like when I meet new people. I can't stop talking. But I'll try to watch myself, Cara, honestly."

"Oh, and Chrissy," Caroline went on, "don't take anyone here too seriously. They take a bit of getting used to, but they're all a lot of fun once you get to know them. They're just a little overpowering at first."

She looked at Chrissy and smiled. Chrissy knew that her cousin's pep talk was as much for Caroline as it was for herself, since Caroline was shy especially around people she didn't know very well.

The people gathered by the pillar contrasted dramatically with the peaceful gloom of the old gym. They were all dressed in bright colors. Chrissy thought they looked like the petals of an exotic flower. There was a girl wearing a scarlet knee-length sweater, and a boy in loud surfer shorts and a huge straw hat. She noticed one girl in an Indian outfit complete with streaming scarves, and another girl with long black hair, wearing a brilliantly painted sweatshirt. Chrissy wondered which was Rainbow and which was Sacha.

"I don't see Mr. Yamagata here yet," Caroline commented. "Do you know any of these kids?"

"I don't see anyone I recognize," Chrissy replied.

"Come on over and I'll introduce you," Caroline said, but Chrissy grabbed her cousin's arm.

"Don't go telling everyone right off that I'm from Iowa," she whispered.

Caroline grinned. "I never thought I'd see the day when you would be shy," she whispered back.

"I'm not shy," Chrissy said. "It's just that I don't want to start out with one strike against me. These kids look as if they might find a farm girl as foreign as a man from Mars."

"I'm sure they're not like that," Caroline said. "They're all kind of sophisticated, but they're nice. And don't worry if they put you down sometimes. They spend a lot of time insulting each other. It's a game for them."

I hope I don't blow it, Chrissy thought as she and her cousin approached the group. She wanted them to like her. *Wouldn't it be great if they invited me to be on the committee with Caroline!*

"Hi, everyone," Caroline called. Six heads turned toward the girls.

"Oh, great. Here's Caroline now," the boy in the surfer shorts said. "Get over here, you're late! We couldn't start any serious work until you arrived."

"Aren't you guys waiting for Mr. Yamagata?" Caroline asked.

The boy stared at her seriously. "Of course not. We were waiting for you to move the bleachers for us."

"Most amusing, Dominic," Caroline said, walking across to put her jacket on the seats. "I hope you guys don't mind, I've brought Chrissy along to help."

"Fantastico!" Dominic said. "She can help move the bleachers, too."

"Okay. Where do you want them?" Chrissy asked brightly.

The other kids burst out laughing. "That was touché to you, Dominic," the girl in the Indian outfit said, applauding.

Chrissy giggled nervously. "You don't really want them moved then?" she asked.

This just made the other kids laugh even more. Chrissy opened her mouth, then shut it again. She didn't see what was funny about the whole thing, but the kids all thought she'd made a joke. How was she to know they were only kidding around?

"Dominic has a thing about the bleachers ruining the whole scene," the girl in the painted sweatshirt said, still looking amused.

"Then let him move them," a dark-haired boy quipped from the shadow behind the pillar.

Dominic looked horrified. "What? And risk damaging my painting arm?" he asked. "You wouldn't make me do that, would you?"

"No, forget about the bleachers, Dom," the girl in the sweatshirt told him. "We've been into it before. They're attached to the floor with rusty iron bolts, and there's no way we can remove them. Let's face the fact that we're stuck with them and get on with it." Sacha paused and looked around. "Now, we have to decide where we're going to put the big folding screen, because everything else has to go around that."

"The light in here is so wonderful, don't you think?" the girl in the Indian outfit remarked to Chrissy.

"Oh, is it?" Chrissy replied. "Shall I go turn it on?"

"Do what?" the girl asked in surprise. Then she giggled. "Mama mia, you do have a dry sense of humor," she said. "I like that."

It took Chrissy a couple of seconds to realize where she had made the mistake this time. The girl wasn't talking about an electric light, but the natural light filtering in through the high windows. Chrissy didn't think the light was wonderful at all. It lit part of the floor in dazzling whiteness and left the rest in gloom. But she gave the girl what she hoped was a sophisticated smile to show that she knew she'd said something amusing.

I'd better shut up, Chrissy thought. *I seem to say something funny each time I open my mouth. Only I'm not trying to be funny.* She moved to the edge of the group, determined to listen rather than speak until she felt more at ease.

The others were all gazing up at the windows.

"Doesn't it remind you of the very white light Vermeer used in his paintings?" the girl in the Indian outfit asked.

"I don't think it's as harsh, Rainbow," Dominic

suggested. "I think it's more an Impressionist light. You know, early Monet?"

"I disagree totally. The whole suggestion of this place is Venetian," another voice chimed in. "Don't you get exactly the same feeling in that palace that's now the Venice post office?"

"That's right, you do," Caroline agreed. "It's the marble and the high windows. Very Venetian."

"That's why Hunter was such a genius to tie this in to the carnival," the girl in the scarlet sweater said.

"That's me, boy genius," the deep voice agreed solemnly. Chrissy stepped forward to try to catch a glimpse of the boy speaking, but he was hidden in the shadow of the pillar. The others laughed at his remark.

"Will you musclemen stop talking and bring in the screen, please," Sacha commanded.

"If you say so, Sacha," one of the boys muttered, and several of them trooped out through a side door, laughing and talking noisily as they went.

"Now we can get down to serious business," Sacha said. "Let's decide which area would be best to display the sculptures. A lot of stuff's already arrived, and we have some pretty delicate multimedia pieces that shouldn't be in a main traffic area."

"Oh, let's see what we've got already," Rainbow begged.

Sacha led the way over to a stack of packages and crates stacked against the wall. The girls pounced on them as if they were presents under a Christmas tree, exclaiming over them with delight or disgust as they opened each one.

"Hey, look at this, doesn't it remind you of Buf-fano?"

"More like buffalo, you mean!"

"I think it's good."

"It is not, Rainbow. How can you call it good? It's so simplistic, it's childish."

"Look at this watercolor, everyone. It's done on handmade paper, isn't it?"

"How symbolic—the San Francisco waterfront, painted on Kleenex tissue!"

More laughter from the group.

Chrissy stood like an extra statue, watching the others. *I'd better keep out of their way, or I'm going to blow it for sure*, she told herself.

The one thing she knew she couldn't do was to join in their conversation. That would only reveal her total ignorance about art and culture. How did these kids know so much? It sounded as if they had visited every art gallery in the world—and actually enjoyed it! Once she'd grown out of the finger painting stage, Chrissy hadn't had much interest in art.

I wish I hadn't come, she thought. *I'm like a fish out of water with these people. How did I ever imagine I'd fit in with them? Just because Cara finds them fun and amusing* . . . Caroline fit in perfectly, Chrissy noticed. She knew all the right things to say, and now she was as excited as the others, busily opening packages. The boys came back carrying the screens and making a big fuss about how heavy they were. But once they saw the artwork being unwrapped, they forgot the screens and joined the others in front of each piece of art.

They've got this all backward, Chrissy thought. *They*

keep talking about the light and displaying the art, but they don't seem to notice that this place is knee deep in dust and trash. The logical thing to do would be to get rid of all this junk and give the floor a darned good sweep before setting up!

But Chrissy didn't dare suggest this. Instead she left the others to continue unpacking, and wandered around, picking up trash as she walked. In a locker room behind the main gym she finally unearthed an old broom and started sweeping. As Chrissy cleared the dust off the floor, she could hear the others arguing over where each piece of art should be displayed.

"But look how this one shines where the sun falls on it," Rainbow was saying as Chrissy began to sweep the far end of the gym. "We have to have it in the middle."

"But we can't just have one piece of sculpture here," Dominic said firmly. "It destroys the symmetry. The long screen should go here and the sculptures over to the left."

"Well, I don't think that's being fair to the artist," Rainbow argued. "After all, he took the trouble to make his work shiny. We should let it shine."

"Let it shine, let it shine," the girl in scarlet sang out.

"Hey, Sacha," another boy commented. "Take a look at this painting. It's just like your sweatshirt!"

Chrissy looked up to see.

"It is not!" Sacha said, tossing back her thick black hair with one long, elegant hand. "I'll have you know my sweatshirt is an original Ragattini."

"Sounds like pasta," came a comment from behind the screen.

"Yeah, that's what your sweatshirt reminds me of —

Fettuccine Alfredo!" another deep voice teased. Everyone laughed but Sacha. She walked away with her head held high.

"Those boys are so juvenile," she said, coming over to Chrissy. "I don't know how we're going to get any work done with them around. And I have to be out of here by one o'clock." Sacha paused and adjusted her sweatshirt. "I'm going to try and get in to *Traviata*."

"Oh, really?" Chrissy said. She was about to ask if *Traviata* was a popular restaurant, but decided she'd better keep her mouth shut.

"I hope there are seats left," Sacha continued. "I couldn't bear to miss *La Traviata*. It's my absolutely favorite opera." Sacha suddenly noticed Chrissy still sweeping, and started coughing dramatically. "Hey, don't do that now," she commanded. "You'll get dust all over the exhibits. Look, it's flying everywhere."

Chrissy stopped sweeping. She wanted to say that if they left the floor in this condition, the exhibits would get dusty every time anyone walked past. But Chrissy looked at Sacha's stern face and decided that she wouldn't be wise to get on the wrong side of her. She put down the broom.

"Look at this everyone. Isn't this powerful stuff?" Dominic called. He held up a huge painting. It was so huge, Chrissy couldn't even see Dominic behind the canvas. It looked to Chrissy as if someone had thrown some paint at the canvas, then ridden over it on a motorbike. "What statement does it make to you?" Dominic asked the group. They all seemed to have something to say. Chrissy was terrified someone would ask her opinion, so she slipped behind the bleachers and began picking up the piles of trash there.

This was the dirtiest part of the gym. It looked as if hundreds of Maxwell students had dropped empty soda cans under the bleachers throughout generations of games, and no one had ever cleared them away. Chrissy began picking up the cans by the armful, but she couldn't find anything to put them in. She certainly didn't want to interrupt the others to ask, so she made a game of stacking the cans in piles.

She remembered how she had loved to build towers like this when she was little. Chrissy and her brother Will used to creep into their mother's kitchen cupboards and see who could build the biggest towers with all the cans and jars. Will usually won because Chrissy was too impatient. But now she made sure her towers didn't fall down. By first building a firm base of cans, Chrissy created a pyramid, making fun patterns with the different colored cans.

I'd better take this down before the other kids notice it, she thought. *If they think their own friends are juvenile, they'll probably think I should be back in kindergarten! I wonder if they've finished unpacking?*

She turned away from her tower to find herself looking into the eyes of the most gorgeous boy she'd ever seen. She had noticed him earlier, lounging easily against one of the pillars, but hidden by a shadow. From a distance she hadn't been aware of his magnetism, but now she felt it powerfully. He was tall, with large dark eyes and curly dark hair. Most of his hair fell neatly into place, but one curl had fallen across his forehead. He wore a brilliant paisley shirt in red and blue, and his jeans were held up by yellow suspenders. Somehow the unusual outfit didn't look strange on him—in fact, it suited him perfectly. As he smiled at Chrissy, his dark eyes lit up, and she felt her knees turn to jelly.

"Hi," he said, and Chrissy recognized the deep laughing voice that she had heard teasing Sacha. "Did you do this?" he asked, looking at her tower of cans.

Wonderful! Chrissy thought in despair. *I come face to face with the most gorgeous guy on this planet and he catches me acting like a little kid. That's a sure way to impress a guy!*

For once Chrissy was tongue-tied. "I just wanted to . . ." she stammered. "You see, I couldn't find . . ."

Her lips and her tongue wouldn't obey her. She realized that she was sounding like an idiot.

The boy didn't seem to notice. He turned his gaze back to her tower of cans. "Very interesting," he remarked. "In fact, it's probably the most original thing I've seen today."

Chrissy wondered which of them was going bananas. She glanced around, but couldn't figure out what it was the boy thought so original.

"Er . . . excuse me?" she mumbled. *What witty conversation, Chrissy Madden!* she thought in despair. *He'll think you're the biggest moron he's ever met!*

The boy went on smiling easily. "The sculpture, I mean," he said, pointing to Chrissy's tower. "What a neat idea—to do a sculpture with old cans. What do you call it?"

Chrissy opened her mouth again. "But it's not . . ." she mumbled. "You see, I only . . ."

Then the boy laughed, his eyes creasing at the sides

in a way Chrissy found extremely attractive. "You're too modest," he said. "When I do something good, I yell about it to the whole world. I'm Hunter, by the way. And I can't believe that I haven't met you around school before."

"I'm Chrissy," she stammered. "I only arrived this semester."

"That explains it, then," Hunter said. "I missed the first two weeks of this semester because the yacht we were on got a big hole in the bottom, so we had to stay an extra two weeks in Tahiti. Wasn't that tragic?" He laughed again. Chrissy thought it was the nicest, warmest laugh she'd ever heard.

"Very tragic," she agreed. "Are you sure you didn't make the hole yourself?"

Hunter laughed harder. "You want to hear a really sad story?" he asked. "That guy in the shorts—Dominic—he went to visit relatives in the midwest this summer, and he came down with chickenpox there. Can you imagine having to spend an extra two weeks in Nebraska or some other place in the boonies?" He paused to smile at Chrissy again, then asked, "Where are you from?"

"Me?" It came out as a squeak. "Well, I'm from . . . er, different places. . . ."

"Like where?"

Chrissy's mind raced desperately. *Anywhere but Iowa*, she kept reminding herself. "Oh, all over," she stammered.

"Sounds interesting," Hunter said with his bewitching smile. "Your father must be in the military, I suppose. They're always on the move."

"Er, yes, that's it. My father's in the military." The words tumbled out in a rush.

"See, I knew it," Hunter said triumphantly. "What rank?"

"Oh, well he's . . ." Why couldn't she think of any military ranks?"

"I bet he's a general or something and you're too modest to admit it."

"Something like that," Chrissy mumbled. The conversation was getting totally out of hand.

"Well, what's your last name—I've met a few generals, maybe I've met your father. Is he stationed in San Francisco right now?"

Chrissy was feeling more and more trapped. "Oh, no, I'm just staying here with my cousin. You see, my parents are . . . far away right now."

"Abroad?"

"That's it. Abroad."

"In Europe?"

"That's right. Europe."

"How neat. No wonder you're so creative. Art in Europe is way ahead of art here, isn't it?"

"I guess so," Chrissy said softly, feeling unhappy and confused. *This stupid charade has got to stop. Tell him right now you're a farm girl from Iowa*, she commanded herself.

But Hunter leaned toward her and rested his hand on her arm. His touch felt warm through the sleeve of her blouse. "Hey, listen, Chrissy. Would you like to come to a party tonight?"

Chrissy had just opened her mouth to tell him that she wasn't a general's daughter who'd recently moved from

Europe, but instead she heard herself saying, "I'd love to come, thank you."

Hunter beamed. "Great! I'll pick you up around eight, then. Write down your address for me on this sheet of paper."

What are you doing? Chrissy asked herself as she printed her address for him. *Have you completely lost your mind? You've just agreed to go to a party with a guy who thinks you're a general's daughter who builds sculptures and tours Europe.*

I can't help it, she argued back. *He is the most gorgeous boy I've ever met, and I'd be a fool to turn him down.*

You're a big phony Chrissy Madden, her conscience scolded.

But it's just for a little while, she replied. *I'll tell him the truth when the time is right. Once he finds out what a nice, fun person I am, then I'll tell him I'm not an artist from Europe, but just a country girl from Iowa.*

Chapter 5

"Phew, thank heavens that's over," Caroline exclaimed, stepping out of the gym and into the open air. "I've breathed enough dust to clog both lungs. I don't know why we all didn't sweep the place out first. Mr. Yamagata says they're going to bring in the big industrial vacuum cleaner on Monday and that should take care of it. I hope it doesn't swallow any of the exhibits!" She started to giggle. "Chrissy, can you picture the vacuum cleaner gulping down that soft sculpture that looks like an octopus? One big slurp and it would disappear!"

She paused and looked at Chrissy. "You're very quiet, especially for you," she said. "I guess that group wasn't really your cup of tea after all. Were you very bored?"

Chrissy blinked in the strong sunlight, still dazed by her experience of the last half hour. She smiled at Caroline and shook her head.

"Amazing," Caroline said, staring at her cousin. "I

don't think I've ever seen you at a loss for words. I always imagined that if Prince Charles and Lady Di came to visit, you'd be the first one to go over and say, 'Hi there, Chuck, how's it going!'"

Chrissy attempted to give her cousin a withering look. Caroline giggled. "Are you okay?" she asked. "I mean, you're not suffering from dust poisoning or something? You do have a weird look on your face."

Chrissy took a deep breath. "That's because I still haven't pulled myself together after what happened in the gym."

"What happened?" Caroline asked in alarm.

Chrissy smiled from ear to ear. "Hunter invited me to a party tonight."

"Hunter? Hunter Bryce invited you to a party?" Caroline almost yelled.

"I know, I can't get over it, either," Chrissy said. "Isn't he the most gorgeous guy you've ever seen?"

"Not *the* most gorgeous, maybe," Caroline said thoughtfully. "But certainly one of the most gorgeous. He really is a babe. I have to admit that. But don't go falling for him too hard, okay, Chrissy? I don't want you getting hurt."

"I'm only going to a party with him," Chrissy said. "I don't intend to fall for him. After all, I have got Ben at home, you know."

"Yes, I know, Chrissy. What about poor old Ben? Do you think he'd understand if you went out with the biggest babe in San Francisco?"

Chrissy sighed. "Well," she said, then hesitated. "We did agree before I left that we could date other people if we wanted. And I couldn't turn down a chance like this, could I, Cara? I'll finally fit in here because I'm me, not because I'm your cousin. I've been here two months now, and for most of that time I've been tagging along with you and your friends."

"You haven't been tagging along, Chrissy," Caroline said hastily. "We all like your company."

"Even so," Chrissy said, "when we go out, everyone is a couple except me. I can't help feeling left out when I watch everyone else walk along in pairs, holding hands, and me the oddball." She turned and looked at her cousin. "I feel like an observer, Cara," she said. "And I'm not used to sitting on the sidelines, watching other people have a good time."

Caroline looked at Chrissy with a hurt expression. "But Chrissy, I thought you were having a good time, too."

"Oh, I am, Cara," Chrissy consoled her cousin. "What I meant was, having a good time with someone special—like you and Alex. That's why this will be so good for me. Through Hunter I'll have a life of my own here. I won't have to wait for you and Alex to be so kind to me. . . ."

Caroline nodded. "I understand, Chrissy," she said. "I only hope you're not playing with fire. Do you think you can handle a guy like Hunter?"

Chrissy grinned suddenly, her whole face lighting up. "You should see me wrestle with the hogs at home. I hold them down and then I tag them on the ear. I don't think I'll have any problems with a guy."

"I wasn't thinking so much of physical problems as emotional ones," Caroline said thoughtfully. "You're not used to guys like Hunter, who plays games with words, and with feelings, too. He's grown up pretty spoiled, I imagine. His parents are on the San Francisco Arts Council and give these huge parties for the symphony and the opera, so they must be really rich. I know he leads a very sophisticated life."

"Hey, wait a minute," Chrissy said, bouncing back to her normal loud self. "I'm not intending to marry the guy. I've just agreed to go to a party with him. Come on, Cara, would you turn down the opportunity to go out with a guy like Hunter? I've been plodding along with good old Ben for three years now. I've got to have some excitement just once in my life, don't I?"

Caroline laughed. "Sure, Chrissy," she said. "And don't think I'm trying to scare you off. Hunter seems okay, and I'm sure he's a very nice person. He's got a great sense of humor and he's lots of fun. I just thought you might be out of your league going to the sorts of parties he goes to and mixing with his crowd."

"I'll give it a whirl," Chrissy said, still grinning. "Even if he finds out after one evening that I'm a little hick from Iowa, I'll have had one great time gazing into those gorgeous brown eyes!"

Caroline looked at Chrissy with admiration. "You're pretty tough, you know that?" she said. "I don't think I'd have the nerve to go out with a guy like Hunter, because I could see how easy it would be to fall for him in a big way."

"Not me," Chrissy said firmly. "He sure is gorgeous, super cute, and a total babe, but I also know that he'd make a terrible long-term boyfriend. And besides, I'm more than happy with Ben back home. Now, will you stop worrying about me and help me decide what to wear tonight?"

"Hmm, what should you wear? Hunter's sure to notice," Caroline said.

Both girls lapsed into silence. Chrissy mentally went through her wardrobe and decided that everything she owned was totally wrong for the party with Hunter. She had seen the trendy outfits people wore that morning. People like that would laugh at her frilly lace dress or her denim skirt with the checked shirt—clothes people at home considered stylish.

"There's nothing really—both girls began together, then both broke off and laughed.

"Maybe something of mine would fit you," Caroline suggested. "You could try my gray overalls."

Chrissy secretly thought that overalls were a strange thing to wear to a party. In Danbury people dressed up for parties and wore overalls for work on the farm.

"Are you sure overalls would be the right thing?" she asked doubtfully.

Caroline considered. "Well, anything goes, really, within reason," she said. "You saw the kids today. Hunter's friends use their clothes to express themselves, but your clothes, well they're just too . . ."

"Too what?" Chrissy demanded.

"Well, they're just too nice. They're crisp and clean but nobody wants to look crisp and clean anymore. Old is beautiful, you know!"

Chrissy giggled. "Dumb, isn't it? It still blows my mind that kids would spend more for a pair of old faded jeans than for a spanking new pair."

"It's just fashion, I guess," Caroline said. "Maybe

you could borrow one of my dad's shirts? Oversized shirts are in right now, or maybe my big sweatshirt, if that won't be too hot. We'll have a try-on session when I get home from ballet, okay?"

"Are you going straight to ballet class now?"

Caroline nodded. "Yeah, it's a little easier. I can skip two hills if I just keep going. I'll pick up a taco or a salad at the deli as I go past."

"But you'll be back this evening to help me get ready for the party, won't you?" Chrissy asked. "Now that I think about it, I'm kind of scared. I don't know what to say or how to act."

"Just don't tell them any stories about the hogs," Caroline said with a grin.

"I wouldn't do that," Chrissy said. "In fact, Hunter doesn't even know that I come from Iowa." She didn't mention to Caroline that Hunter thought she was a general's daughter, fresh from Europe. That small fact would have to be smoothed out later, if this evening went well, Chrissy decided.

"If I were you, I'd just listen and smile a lot," Caroline suggested. "Until you get the feel of their conversation."

"I got the feel of their conversation this morning," Chrissy said, her stomach tying itself into a tight knot as she thought about the sophisticated crowd she would be mingling with that night. "Everything they said was double Dutch to me. They talked about painters I hadn't heard of and places I hadn't been."

Caroline smiled. "Maybe I'd better give you instant sophistication lessons," she suggested. "You know, a crash course on everything you want to know about the arts but were afraid to ask?"

Chrissy laughed. "That would be funny," she said. "I'd have to check my little notes and say to people, 'I'm sorry, I can't discuss Picasso tonight. I don't get to him until lesson three!'"

The girls were still laughing as Caroline waved to Chrissy and turned down Nob Hill toward her dance class downtown. Chrissy stood on top of the hill, feeling the fresh wind from the bay blowing in her face and watching Caroline's graceful strides.

Look how easily she moves, Chrissy thought enviously. *She almost floats. That's why she's a ballerina, I guess. Not like me, clomping along like a clumsy oaf. I hope I don't do anything clumsy tonight, like upset the chips or something. And I hope I don't say wrong things.* Then she thought of Hunter and the way his eyes crinkled when he laughed, and her normal high spirits returned. *Aw, what the heck*, she decided. *They can't talk about art all evening. After all, they are kids and they are human, aren't they? They've got to eat and dance, and I can do both those things better than anybody. I'm not going to worry about it anymore. I'm just going to go and have a good time!*

Chapter 6

Chrissy tingled with excitement as she got ready for the party. It was her first real date in California, after all. And a handsome boy had invited her—out of all the girls at Maxwell High—to go to the party with him!

Maybe this will be the start of something really good, she told herself as she showered. But every time she thought of Hunter, a picture of Ben crept into her mind.

What about Ben? she asked herself, then decided she had no reason to feel guilty. *I'm sure he'd understand. He would expect me to go on dates. Why, I bet he's been going to lots of parties without me, and dancing with other girls.*

She tried not to think of Ben for the rest of the evening. Caroline had come back from ballet class in time to help her get ready, and she had even been nice enough to let Chrissy go through her entire wardrobe to find just the right thing to wear. After trying on everything from a prom dress to an Army camouflage outfit,

Chrissy had chosen a black dress with rhinestone straps that Caroline had worn to a symphony opening the year before, and long rhinestone earrings to go with it. She liked what she saw in the mirror, and Hunter seemed to approve, too, if Chrissy could judge by the sparkle in his eyes when she met him at the door.

He had shown up right on time, looking wonderful in white denims and an open-weave Mexican shirt that accented his tan. When seeing him again, Chrissy experienced all the same symptoms of the morning—weak knees, rapidly beating heart, and a paralyzed mouth. *How can just looking at a boy turn me into a mumbling, stumbling idiot?* she thought, feeling mad at herself for her strange behavior. When she had first started going out with Ben, she'd felt proud and excited, but never in her life had she felt this way!

Hunter bounded down the stairs ahead of Chrissy to open the door of his white Porsche for her. As Chrissy walked around the back of the car to the passenger's seat, she noticed the license plate that said HUNTER in big letters. *Holy mazoley!* she thought in amazement. *This is quite a change from Ben's old pickup!* She began to wonder if she was dreaming, as she sank into the red leather seat of the Porsche. Then Hunter climbed in beside her and gave her hand a squeeze.

"We're going to have a great time tonight," he said. His hand was warm and strong, and Chrissy knew she wasn't dreaming.

Think of Ben, Chrissy told herself firmly. *Don't get too carried away with all this*.

Chrissy felt more comfortable with Hunter as they drove to the party. They chattered on about the art fair and teachers at Maxwell and Hunter's car. By the time they arrived, Chrissy felt much more confident.

She tried her best to fit in at the beginning of the party, but it seemed that the most innocent of conversations was full of pitfalls. They had barely gotten inside the door when they were met by Rainbow, now wearing another Indian outfit, even more stunning than the last one. It was white with little mirrors sewn all over, so that Rainbow sparkled as she walked.

"I really like your clothes," Chrissy said to her as Hunter went to get the drinks. "You must tell me where you get them."

Rainbow gave Chrissy a friendly smile. "Why, thank you," she said. "This comes from the Varanasi Bazaar."

"I must remember to look there the next time I go shopping," Chrissy commented.

Rainbow giggled. "Do you usually do your shopping in India?" she asked. "Now that's what I call jet-setting."

Chrissy had laughed, but that first encounter made her more cautious. *How was I to know that she was talking about a place in India?* Chrissy thought now. She took another sip of mineral water. *Why can't kids in San Francisco have normal parties with sodas and popcorn and dancing, the way we do at home?* she wondered, glancing around at the various groups of people deep in conversation. True, there was music in the background and a few kids had disappeared out to the patio to dance, but most of them were still inside, eating, drinking, and talking.

The drinking had been another problem for Chrissy.

She had tactfully turned down the wine and beer that Hunter offered her, then found to her dismay that there was no soda available. She had ended up taking a bottle of French mineral water instead. Chrissy noticed several of the other kids drinking mineral water too, so she guessed it must be a fashionable thing to do. Thank goodness for that, she thought.

She had spent the last hour or so trying to mingle, mostly listening and smiling—as Caroline had suggested—but always anticipating the tricky questions. It was like taking an exam. She had to think carefully about every word and hope that she'd said the right thing. So far she hadn't done too badly. Hunter had been very sweet and attentive all evening, but Chrissy doubted that his friends would want to include her in their group if she stood quietly with a ridiculous grin pasted on her face all the time.

Now she was squeezed gratefully into a corner behind the food table. The corner was only dimly lit, and Chrissy hoped she might blend into the drapes so she wouldn't be forced to mingle anymore. She took a long drink of the mineral water. It tasted to Chrissy like the medicine her grandmother used to give her when she was "under the weather." Why would anyone drink this stuff when they could have lemonade instead? she wondered. It didn't even quench her thirst as well as lemonade, and she certainly needed her thirst quenched now. It was a warm evening and she felt as clammy as if she'd run a mile.

I feel like a spy, she thought. *It's not easy watching every word I say so no one will discover my secret.*

From the other side of the room Chrissy heard a

burst of laughter. She looked over and saw Hunter in the middle of the crowd. He certainly knew how to enjoy himself. Chrissy got the sense that he was always laughing or smiling. *I wonder if those gorgeous crinkles around his eyes are permanent?* she mused. She'd looked forward to being with him this evening, but now that she was here, she kept looking at her watch, praying that the party would soon be over.

I guess I'd better face it, she thought, *I don't belong here. Maybe I don't belong in the city at all.* Visions of the parties back home kept drifting through her mind. She always enjoyed those parties in rooms packed with wall to wall kids, all dancing and laughing at the same time, and the noise level so high that the house vibrated. Chrissy could even imagine a hutch groaning under its cargo of ham surrounded by pot luck dishes. There was nothing familiar to her as she looked up and down the table at all the exotic foods. *Even the refreshments are different*, she thought.

Another girl wandered over to the table, wearing a pair of black overalls with spiked heels and huge drop earrings. Chrissy recalled Caroline's offer to lend her a pair of gray overalls. She had scoffed then, but somehow the overalls looked good on this girl, Chrissy had to admit. Earlier the girl had talked about her summer in Europe, so Chrissy pretended to be occupied with the food, in case she was asked any questions she couldn't answer. She picked up a leaf from the platter nearest her. It was a thick, fleshy green leaf with a little mayonnaise and a shrimp at its base. Chrissy stuffed it into her mouth.

"I just love artichokes, don't you?" the girl said, smiling at Chrissy.

Chrissy just nodded and smiled back. She couldn't say anything even if she wanted to, because she was busy fighting with a mouthful of spiky, stringy, unchewable leaf. *No wonder they call it an artichoke*, she thought in a panic. *It tries to choke you!* The leaf scratched the inside of her mouth each time she tried to swallow it, and she wondered if an artichoke could be a kind of cactus.

The other girl didn't seem to notice anything wrong. She picked up one of the leaves and ran it between her teeth, scooping off the flesh with the mayonnaise and the shrimp, then dropped the spiky, stringy remains into the wastebasket.

So that's how you're supposed to eat it, Chrissy thought. But it was too late.

"Excuse me," she mumbled and fled outside through the sliding glass doors. In the darkness at the edge of the patio, she managed to spit her artichoke into a napkin and drop it on a tray full of garbage. *I'll die of hunger at this party*, she thought gloomily, deciding not to eat another thing.

"Oh, there you are," Hunter said from behind her. "I was looking all over for you. I thought you'd run off without me."

Chrissy turned to him. "Oh, no," she said. "I just came out for a little fresh air."

Hunter nodded. "It is pretty hot and uncomfortable in there," he agreed. "I hope I wasn't neglecting you. Trevor was just telling us about this girl who used to be in our class. She moved to Paris last year, and he went to visit her this summer. He said she'd turned into a real blimp. She used to be so skinny, too. I guess European food is pretty fattening huh?"

"I guess it is," Chrissy agreed.

"Do you want something to eat now?" he asked.

"Oh, no thanks," Chrissy said hastily, visualizing Hunter's reaction as she tried to decide what to do with various unknown foods. "I'm really not hungry," she lied.

Hunter grinned. "I shouldn't have told you the story," he said. "Now I bet you're self-conscious about the pounds you picked up in Europe! How about dancing some of it off instead?"

He took Chrissy's arm, led her inside, then swept her onto the dance floor. "Hey, Josh, put on something with a beat to it, will you?" he called. "We want to dance, not crawl!"

The music changed to an up-tempo throbbing beat. Hunter started to dance to it and Chrissy quickly picked up his movements. *At least I can dance with the best of them*, she thought. *I should be able to, after all that cheerleading practice last year.* As they danced, she was aware that other couples had stopped to watch them. Hunter moved easily to the music and each time he caught her eye, she could see he was enjoying himself.

"You're a great dancer," he whispered in her ear. "How about teaching me some of the latest dance crazes from London?"

"Oh, I don't go in for dance crazes too much," Chrissy stammered. "I just do what feels right."

"Me too," Hunter agreed. Then the music changed, and Hunter's face lit up. "This is one dance we definitely have to do. Tango, madame?" he asked, and without waiting for a reply, he scooped her into his arms, holding her close to him as he set off down the floor with giant, gliding strides.

Chrissy had seen the tango in old movies, but she'd never tried dancing it! Luckily Hunter was a skillful leader, so Chrissy was quick to learn the steps. She could feel her heart thumping in panic the first couple of times they crossed the floor and spun around, but after that she found the dance exciting. She felt Hunter's bristly cheek pressed against hers as they moved to the rhythm as one, and it was a new sensation for her to dance so closely with a boy. When the music ended, Hunter spun her into the classic back bend, leaning over so their lips were just inches apart.

"I think we make a great couple, don't you?" he asked, helping Chrissy stand upright. "They really knew what they were doing when they invented those old dances. Much more romantic than standing ten feet away from your partner and swinging your arms."

Chrissy had to agree. Ben's idea of dancing was standing in one spot, shaking his shoulders to the fast numbers and swaying with her gently to the slow ones. No dance had ever left her feeling so breathless and confused.

"Do you want to take a break?" Hunter asked.

"Oh, no," Chrissy said hastily. "I love dancing, if you don't feel too tired."

"Me?" Hunter asked. "Lady, I ran the San Francisco marathon last year. I can dance all night if you want to."

So they kept dancing until the party finally broke up

after midnight. Long before that Chrissy's energy had started to fade. She'd found it hard to put one foot in front of the other, but the thought of having to mingle with the other kids, plus the delight of being in Hunter's arms, had kept her on the dance floor.

"Phew, I'm exhausted," Hunter said as he flopped into the car beside her. "You are incredible. I'm going to have to go into training to keep up with you!"

They drove in silence, the streetlights shining in Hunter's warm brown eyes. He slid his right hand from the steering wheel and entwined his fingers with hers, as if it was the most natural thing in the world. Then he went on driving, steering the car easily down the hill with one hand.

At last they pulled up outside her house.

"I had a wonderful evening," Chrissy said. "Thank you for taking me."

"I'm glad you had a good time," Hunter said. "I felt guilty at the beginning of the party because I could see that you were bored. I guess a party like that must seem dull after the parties you went to in Europe. I mean, the people are so ordinary here. I bet you're used to a really sophisticated, artistic crowd, aren't you?"

"I'm always a little quiet in a room full of new people," Chrissy said hastily, "and I wasn't bored with you. I loved dancing with you, Hunter."

"I certainly wasn't bored with you, either, Chrissy," Hunter said. Chrissy could sense that he was going to kiss her, and she knew she should get out of the car in a hurry. But she hesitated for a moment, then Hunter took her in his arms and brought his lips to hers. His kiss was so warm and overpowering that thoughts of anything else floated far away from Chrissy's mind. She found herself relaxing in his embrace and enjoying his kiss.

She didn't know how much time had passed before she finally ran up the stairs to the front door, no longer tired and taking the steps two at a time.

Chapter 7

Chrissy shut the door quietly and leaned against the cool wood, breathing hard from her climb up the stairs.

"I don't believe it," she whispered to herself. "I just don't believe this is happening to me." She put her hand to her lips, remembering the feel of Hunter's kisses. *Could I be falling in love?* she wondered. *I've never felt this way before, not even the first time Ben kissed me....*

The thought of Ben brought her back to reality. Ben! What about Ben? She really hadn't intended to get involved with Hunter. He was only supposed to be a glamorous date, a way to get in with a crowd at school. But Chrissy had to admit that she'd been wildly attracted to him from the first moment he gazed into her eyes the previous morning.

She crept down the hall and opened the door of the bedroom she and Caroline shared. Her cousin was sleeping peacefully, lying on her back beneath neat covers. *She even looks elegant asleep*, Chrissy thought in amazement. Then she reached for the photo on her dresser and sat down on her bed, staring at it, trying to get her thoughts in order. The hall light illuminated Ben's open, friendly face, smiling back at her from inside the wooden frame.

Oh, Ben, she thought. *What am I supposed to do now? You are so special to me, and I do love you, but you're so far away.* And she knew that nothing like Hunter had ever happened to her before. He was so different from anyone she'd ever met.

Chrissy held the photo closer, so that she could study Ben's features—the bright blue eyes which always looked mildly surprised, the tooth that was chipped in one corner from a Pop Warner football game, and the tuft of hair he never quite managed to slick down. She knew everything about that face, even without looking at his picture. *That's part of the trouble*, she thought. *I'm comfortable with him. He's been around so long, but I'm just not sure anymore if he's the right person for me. He's just always been there, that's all.*

She remembered a conversation she'd had with her mother before she made up her mind to come to California. "If you do decide to marry and settle down here in Iowa, I want you to be absolutely sure you are doing the right thing," her mother had said. At that time Chrissy didn't know what her mother meant. She'd been sure that life with Ben in Danbury was the right thing. But now she understood.

Chrissy clasped the photo frame tightly in her hands. *You do understand, don't you, Ben?* she asked the picture silently. *I can't stop seeing Hunter, not yet. I really want to see him again. I want him to kiss me again. I don't know, maybe I'll get over him pretty soon, and maybe then I'll know for sure that I want to spend my life back home with someone like you—but I have to find out for sure. I owe that much to myself, Ben.*

Gently Chrissy put the picture back on the dresser and sat in the half darkness, staring at the floor. "Well, I feel better now," she whispered. "Ben, I hope you understand." But already her thoughts were drifting back to Hunter. *I wonder what's in store for me now? I wonder—.* She stopped short, opening her mouth in horror. "Chrissy Madden," she said to herself severely, "what's gotten into you? You don't know the first thing about the glamorous life he leads!" What if he took her to art galleries, high-brow plays, and expensive restaurants? she wondered. He'd soon find out that she wasn't the girl he thought she was, but a total phony!"

Caroline stirred in her sleep, and Chrissy glanced across at her. As she looked at her cousin, she remembered what Caroline had said that afternoon: "I'd better give you a crash course in sophistication." She had been joking, of course, and Chrissy had laughed, too. Now it didn't seem so dumb after all.

If I just knew enough to get by, Chrissy thought desperately, *maybe he'd never find out about me. . . . I could tell him that he'd made a mistake about Europe, but he doesn't need to know that I'm a farm girl from Iowa.* She looked at Caroline again. *I wonder if she'd really help me if I asked her? I bet she knows all the right things to say and do. It would be perfect. I'd be able to talk about art and food, and know what clothes to wear. Then I'd really fit in with Hunter and his friends.*

Chrissy felt a sense of urgency, and knew she couldn't wait for the morning to talk to her cousin. She stared at Caroline, silently commanding her to wake. Then she bounced around a bit on her bed, hoping that the creeking might wake her. She even coughed a couple of times, but Caroline's expression did not change. Finally, Chrissy leaped up and landed on the end of Caroline's bed. Caroline opened her eyes wide in surprise.

"Chrissy, what on earth?" she murmured. "What time is it?"

"The middle of the night," Chrissy whispered back. "I'm sorry to wake you, but I couldn't wait another minute to ask you something really important."

"What is it?" Caroline mumbled, her eyes already closing again.

"I want to know if you'll give me sophistication lessons, like you said."

"You what?" Caroline asked, her eyes open again.

"You know, what you said today—that I needed a crash course in sophistication. Well, will you give me lessons, Caroline? Please?"

"But Chrissy, I was only joking," Caroline said. She propped herself up on one elbow and looked at her cousin. "How did the date go?"

"Caroline, it was wonderful." Chrissy sighed. "Hunter was just wonderful. Everything was totally wonderful."

"I get the message," Caroline said dryly.

"So you see," Chrissy went on, "I can't risk putting my foot in my mouth now, can I? I don't want him to find out that I don't know anything about anything."

"But Chrissy, be reasonable. I can't teach you how

to behave in a whole different way in a few lessons. Hunter was brought up in a totally different world. Just be yourself with him. If he enjoys your company, I'm sure it's because of the personality you already have."

"But he thinks I've lived in Europe and that I'm artistic," Chrissy said miserably.

"Why would he think things like that?" Caroline asked suspiciously. "Is that what you told him?"

"No, of course not!" Chrissy replied hotly. "You know how I feel about lying. It was a mix-up. He kept answering his own questions about me. Like he'd ask me where I was from, and before I got a chance to answer, he'd say, 'Europe, right?' Well, what could I say? After that we got along so well that now I'm scared to tell him the truth."

"Oh, Chrissy," Caroline said with a sigh. "How do you get yourself into these messes?"

"Things just happen to me, I guess," Chrissy said. "But this time it's one of the most wonderful things that ever happened to anyone! Imagine me with Hunter Bryce, Caroline—isn't that about the most wonderful thing that could happen to anybody?"

Caroline nodded. "I guess it is pretty special. But what about Ben, Chrissy? Have you forgotten him already?"

"Of course I haven't forgotten him," Chrissy said hastily. "It's just that, well, Ben is different. He's like the same old clothes you put on every day. I think I love him, but if I really loved him, would Hunter make me feel like this?"

"How does Hunter make you feel?" Caroline asked with a grin.

"I feel like I'm floating, Cara," Chrissy said. "I ran up the steps, and I swear my feet didn't even touch the ground. Of course, I felt good when I was with Ben, but he never made me feel the way I did when Hunter kissed me. I got goose bumps all over. It was about the most amazing thing that's happened to me in my entire life!" She paused and looked at Caroline. "Tell me, Cara, do you get goose bumps with Alex?"

"No," Caroline said thoughtfully. "I like being with him, and I like it when he kisses me, but I have to admit, he doesn't give me goose bumps."

"Oh," Chrissy said in surprise. "Well, I have to go for it, don't I? How can I let the one big love of my life slip away because I think Picasso is Mexican food?"

Caroline laughed. "Oh, Chrissy," she said. "My life was so peaceful until you arrived."

"You see, I've brought you a little excitement!"

"Try headaches," Caroline said, laughing. "I don't know what you think I can do for you. . . ."

"Do you remember that play we saw downtown— *My Fair Lady?*" Chrissy asked. "You be Professor Higgins and I'll be Eliza Doolittle. You can teach me how to be a proper lady."

"You want me to teach you to say 'The rain in Spain stays mainly in the plain?'"

Chrissy ignored her cousin's sarcasm. "I want to know about things like not eating the whole artichoke."

Caroline laughed. "Oh, Chrissy, only a dummy would think of eating—" She broke off and looked at Chrissy in astonishment. "Chrissy, you didn't?"

"I most certainly did."

"You tried to eat a whole artichoke?"

"Yes, and believe me, it wasn't too funny! It felt like I had a porcupine in my mouth."

"So you've also tried eating porcupines? Boy, you do like to live dangerously."

"Very funny. Of course I've never eaten a porcupine. But I'd never tried an artichoke, either, until tonight. How was I supposed to know what to do with it?" Chrissy's voice became serious. "That's the kind of situation I want to avoid, Cara. Imagine if Hunter took me out to dinner, or to meet his family, and I did something like that. I'd die of embarrassment."

Caroline nodded. "I can see that."

"So you've got to help me, Cara," Chrissy pleaded. "Tell me about food and art and plays and famous cities abroad and the right clothes to wear—"

"All in two easy lessons?" Caroline finished for her. "Chrissy, there's no way I could do any more than scrape the surface. Even if I told you the names of ten painters, I couldn't give you their entire life histories and show you all their famous paintings. And besides, I don't know everything."

"But anything would help, Cara," Chrissy begged. "I just need enough to get by. You said yourself when I first started school that I'd have to learn not to act weird. Well, I'm a lot better already, aren't I? I don't talk about the hogs on the farm anymore, and I sort of know what I should be saying—I just need the right words."

Caroline looked at her cousin before she spoke. "Well, I guess I could help you with clothes, and with food, too, and I could tell you a bit about the places in Europe I've been. But I don't feel good about this,

Chrissy. How long do you think you can pretend to be somebody you're not? In the end you're going to be caught, and then you'll look like a fool. I don't want that to happen to you."

"I'm willing to take the risk, Cara," Chrissy said quietly. "Right now I'm willing to take any risk to see Hunter again. He might end up to be the big love of my life, and I don't want to blow it."

Caroline laughed. "I can't see Hunter being the big love of anybody's life for more than a couple of weeks. He's not the faithful type, Chrissy, so don't go hoping for too much."

"I'm not hoping for too much," Chrissy said with a sigh. "I'm going to be very realistic about the whole thing. But just a couple of weeks with Hunter would be something I could look back on all my life. I just want to be Hunter's kind of girl for a little while. What's wrong with that?"

"It's not wrong," Caroline said, "and I don't want you to think I'm judging you, Chrissy. I don't want you to get hurt. But I can see that you're going to go out with Hunter again no matter what I say, so I suppose I'd better give you my Instant Sophistication Course even if I think it's the craziest idea in the world!"

Chrissy flung her arms around Caroline. "You're terrific, Cara. You're better than any sister. You won't regret this, I promise, and if you ever need me to do a special favor for you, I'll do anything."

With an embarrassed laugh, Caroline fended off her cousin. "Can I have that in writing?" she asked. "Now please, can we go back to sleep? Hunter will not want to date someone with bags under her eyes. Come to think of it, I don't want bags under my eyes, either!"

"Okay, Cara," Chrissy said, sliding from Cara's bed. "Sorry I woke you."

Caroline shook her head, laughing. "You're not sorry at all."

Chrissy laughed, too. "You're right," she said. "I'm not. But I'm going to let you get right back to sleep again, because I'm going to wake you real early to start my training!"

"Chrissy, it's Sunday morning!"

"Don't worry, I'll let you sleep in until at least seven," Chrissy said, then giggled as Caroline opened her eyes wide in horror. "Just kidding," she said. "Go back to sleep. I really meant seven-thirty."

This time Caroline flung a pillow at Chrissy before pulling the covers over her head.

Chapter 8

"So what do you want to do first?" Caroline asked the next morning.

"Eat breakfast," Chrissy said. "It's nearly nine o'clock, and I'm starving. You want me to fry you a couple of eggs?"

"Mama mia!" Carolina said. "How you can face all that food first thing in the morning, I don't know!"

Chrissy grinned. "It's easy. In fact, two eggs is a small breakfast for me. Back home I'd be having a stack of pancakes, four or five pieces of bacon, plus eggs to go with it."

"I know, you've told me," Caroline said. "You go cook your eggs while I take a shower. Then we'll start on the New Improved Christina Madden campaign."

A shadow of doubt crossed Chrissy's face. "Do you think I should start calling myself Christina?" she asked.

"No, I don't," Caroline said quickly. "You look like a perfect Chrissy, not like a Christina at all."

"But by the end of your training do you think maybe I'll be a Christina?" Chrissy asked.

"Don't try fooling with your name, Chrissy," Caroline advised. "Everyone already knows you as Chrissy. It would only call attention to the fact that you want to change your image if you changed names, too. You want people to think you've had the cool image all along."

"That's right, I do," Chrissy agreed. "Oh, well, Chrissy sounds like a fun sort of name, doesn't it? I'm going to go fix my breakfast!" She headed toward the bedroom door. "See ya later, alligator!"

"That's the first thing we've got to change," Caroline said, grinning. "Girls in Hunter's crowd don't say things like that. When you leave a room, you say *ciao!* That's Italian for good-bye."

"Chow!" Chrissy said, as if testing the word for suitability. "Chow!" she said again, this time with a little more drama. Then she called "Chow, darlings!" as she flung out her arm in an extravagant wave, catching the tips of her fingers in the robes hanging on the back of the door. Chrissy stood by the door, her arms outstretched, with two fluffy bathrobes dangling from her hand.

Caroline couldn't help laughing. "Oh, yes, very elegant," she remarked. "Every well-dressed woman wears a pair of bathrobes on her hand. Much more fashionable than rings!"

Chrissy glared at her cousin, shook off the robes, and went out the door with her nose in the air.

"I'm sorry if I laughed," Caroline said ten minutes later, as she came into the kitchen, wearing one of the offending bathrobes, her hair hidden under an enormous white towel. "But you looked so funny."

"That's just what I'm scared of, Cara," Chrissy said, pausing with her fork in midair. "Things like that always happen to me, and I'm scared of making a fool of myself in front of Hunter."

"You've always been able to laugh at yourself before," Caroline said. "Everyone admires your good-natured attitude. I bet Hunter would laugh if you laughed first. He'd like you for it, too."

"I hope so," Chrissy said. "If I can just get through a couple of dates acting really cool and sophisticated, then I won't care. Anything can happen after that."

"So when are you seeing him again? Did he say?" Caroline asked.

"He mentioned something about a concert," Chrissy answered as she took another bite of her fried egg. "But he told me he'd call today. I should be prepared for anything."

"Well, let's start with food, since I know that's one of your main interests," Caroline said, sitting down beside Chrissy and pouring some granola into a bowl. "Now, if he takes you out to eat anywhere special, I'd guess it would be Italian or seafood. Those are the San Francisco specialties. You should try Fettuccine Alfredo, Chrissy. It's absolutely delicious."

"What is it?" Chrissy asked suspiciously.

"It's just fettuccine in a cream sauce with basil." Caroline crunched her granola.

"It's what?"

"Noodles and herbs."

"Oh. Sounds boring," Chrissy said.

"Mmm, it's really good," Caroline replied, swallowing her granola.

"Well, what if he takes me to a seafood place?" Chrissy asked.

"Then the calamari is a good bet," Caroline replied.

"What's that?"

"Squid."

"Squid?"

"Yes, you know, like an octopus."

Chrissy's eyes opened wide in horror. "You mean people eat them?"

"Sure, they're delicious. They cut the mantle into little rings—"

"The what?" Chrissy exclaimed, looking at the remains on her breakfast plate in disgust.

"The head. They cut it into little rings—"

"Yuck! Don't go on, Caroline. I'll stick with noodles and herbs."

"Well, at least you'll know what calamari is if Hunter orders it for you," Caroline replied, pushing her empty bowl aside.

"I think I'd get sick if I had to eat squid's head," Chrissy said, scrunching up her face. "But thanks, I'll write those things down anyway." She picked up a small notebook from the table. "I'm going to keep a little book with all your useful tips in it. Now I can write—what was that stuff called again?"

Caroline told her, and she wrote it down carefully. "Okay. Tell me about more food. Are there other tricky things like artichokes I should know about?"

Caroline laughed. "I can't think of any."

"You mean I picked the one kind of food that's impossible to eat? Boy, what a dummy I am."

Caroline looked at her cousin with understanding. "You're not a dummy at all. I bet there are plenty of things in Iowa that would be completely new to me."

"Not you—you're a world traveler. I bet you know everything about everything," Chrissy said warmly.

"I wish," Caroline said. "The one thing I haven't learned yet is how to stop being shy. I still freak out when I see a room full of people. When we walked into the gym yesterday, I bet I was more nervous than you were, and I knew everybody."

"I've got an idea," Chrissy said. "I'll give you anti-shy lessons while you give me my sophistication lessons!"

"Sounds great," Caroline said. "What's lesson one in anti-shy?"

"I'd have to think about that," Chrissy said seriously. "I suppose it's realizing that everyone else is a person, too—that everyone is afraid of something. It makes people easier to face." She paused to take a sip of milk. "Until I came here, I never felt shy at all. I always took it for granted that everyone was going to like me, I guess. There have been some times here when I've felt shy and out of place, like at that party last night. But somehow everybody usually turns out to be pretty nice."

"You're lucky," Caroline said. "You're the sort of person people automatically like. No, Chrissy, I'm afraid there's no magic cure for my shyness. I just have to make myself get over it." She got up and put her breakfast bowl into the dishwasher. "Come on, let's take another look at your clothes and see if we can come up with some super-cool outfits."

Chrissy mopped up the last of her egg yolk with her bread, then put the empty plate in the dishwasher and followed Caroline into the bedroom.

"That's another problem," she called after Caroline. "I went through my entire wardrobe at least ten times before you woke up this morning and I don't have anything that's even the *least* bit sophisticated. Everything I own makes me look like a little country girl."

"You can borrow some of my things," Caroline said generously. "And we can go raid my dad's closet. Maybe one of his huge sweaters would look good on you, or maybe even his sports jacket."

"Won't he mind?"

"He won't even notice," Caroline said. "He practically lives in that one pair of cords. I bet he doesn't even know what he has hanging up in there."

"Gee, I don't know," Chrissy began, when their conversation was interrupted by the ringing of the telephone.

Caroline bounded to answer it before the noise could wake her parents. Seconds later she returned to the bedroom. "It's for you," she whispered with a big grin on her face. "Hunter certainly doesn't waste any time!"

"It's Hunter?" Chrissy squeaked, leaping up from her bed.

Caroline nodded. "You really must have made a big impression on him."

Chrissy barely heard Caroline's last words as she rushed down the hall to pick up the telephone.

"I hope I didn't wake you." Hunter's deep, rich voice sounded even nicer on the phone.

"Oh, no, I'm used to getting up early," Chrissy said.

"Why back home we—" She stopped, realizing that she had nearly ruined her sophistication image. She'd had such a good time with Hunter last night that she was no longer on her guard.

But Hunter didn't seem to notice anything wrong. "I know," he chuckled. "Military discipline. I bet you had to march to breakfast."

"Not exactly," Chrissy said uncomfortably. *Why don't I come right out and tell him now?* she argued with herself. *I can't go on pretending. I don't feel very good about this. I've got to tell him that I'm not a general's daughter and I've never been to Europe.* But when she tried to form a sentence, her mouth felt dry and she couldn't make any words come out.

"I had a great time last night," Hunter said.

Chrissy took a deep breath. "So did I."

"I wondered," Hunter began, "whether you're busy today. You see, there's an outdoor art fair in the park this morning, and it's a beautiful day for a walk. We could go to the park and then have some lunch, maybe. I'm afraid I have to tag along with my parents this evening, so I only have the first part of the day free. Can you make it?"

"Oh, sure," Chrissy said. "I'd like that."

"Great!" Hunter boomed on the phone. "I'll pick you up in half an hour. Is that too soon?"

"Oh, no, that's just fine," Chrissy said.

The moment Hunter said good-bye, she rushed back to Caroline. "Quick, help me! He's picking me up in half an hour and we're going to an art fair! Tell me the names of some modern artists and what's the art gallery called in London and what on earth shall I wear?"

"I wasn't expecting to give you the entire course in ten minutes," Caroline said dryly. "And you don't have to talk about art just because you're at an art show. Remember, you've already seen the work of Fernando at the reception here last month, so you can talk about him."

"You mean the guy whose sculptures looked like motorbike engines?"

"That's the one."

"But he was awful," Chrissy said as she brushed her long blond hair.

"He's also a very popular modern artist, so watch what you say about him. If you don't like really modern stuff, then talk about the Impressionist exhibition," Caroline suggested. "Remember, you were looking through the catalogue on the coffee table."

"Oh, I remember that. Those paintings were pretty."

"But you don't call something pretty when you're talking about art," Caroline warned. "Say it's charming if it's sort of sweet and gentle, powerful if it's bold and bright, creative if you don't understand what it's about, and interesting if you downright hate it. Got those?"

"Charming, powerful, creative, or interesting. Got it," Chrissy said with a grin. "I think I can get by with those. But what can I wear?"

"Let's see, for an art fair in the park I think my dad's blue sweater with black stirrup pants would look nice," Caroline advised.

"But your dad's still asleep."

"That's okay, you can just creep into his closet and get it."

"I'm not creeping into your parents' closet! You do it!"

"You're the one who's going to wear the sweater!"

"It was your idea!"

A head poked around the door. "Everything okay, girls?" Caroline's father asked. The girls looked at each other.

"Just a friendly discussion," Caroline mumbled.

"Can I help sort it out?" her father asked.

Chrissy coughed.

"No, that's all right, Dad," Caroline said hastily.

Her father shrugged his shoulders. "Okay. I can see when I'm not wanted," he said. "I'll go make some breakfast. Anyone for pancakes?"

"We've already eaten, thanks, and Chrissy has a date in half an hour," Caroline said.

"Okay," he said, turning to go.

"Uncle Richard, I was wondering," Chrissy called after him. "Do you think I could borrow your big blue sweater?"

"Is that the latest craze?" He looked amused. "Well, I don't see why not. Go ahead, it's in my closet."

"See, it was easy," Chrissy said in triumph as she carried the sweater back to Caroline. She slipped it on. "It's so big," she commented, staring at herself in the mirror. The sweater fell to her knees, and the sleeves dangled several inches past Chrissy's hands.

"That's in fashion," Caroline said. "Here, put on my stirrup pants."

Chrissy slipped her legs in, then slowly pulled them up to her hips. "Caroline, I can't get the zipper up," she said in a small voice.

"Oh, I thought we were the same size," Caroline replied.

"We were almost," Chrissy said in horror. "I guess I must have put on weight. I thought my jeans were extra tight lately."

"Well, you do eat a lot," Caroline remarked.

Chrissy groaned. "I've always eaten a lot, but I've always been a size seven."

"Back home you got a lot more exercise. Now you're eating the same amount without the same exercise."

"You're right," Chrissy said. "Tell me honestly, am I too fat?"

"Maybe a little," Caroline admitted. "But you've got fairly big bones."

"With a little chub on top of them?" Chrissy asked, trying to laugh. She thought for a moment. "Come to think of it, Hunter did mention something about picking up extra pounds. I wonder if he meant me? Caroline, do you think I should go on a diet?"

"Maybe five pounds or so," Caroline said. "If you want to wear more of my clothes, that is. You can probably just use a safety pin to hold those pants together."

Frowning, Chrissy rummaged through the dresser for a safety pin. "I love food," she said, her frown turning into a grin. "I don't know if I could survive on cottage cheese and celery sticks, but I don't want to turn into a blimp, and I do want Hunter to like me, so I guess that's that. If you have a few minutes today, Cara, would you plan out a diet sheet for me, and maybe a list of all the art galleries in the world, painters since the year one, every opera ever written, and the complete history of classical music?"

"Get out of here," Caroline said, laughing and threatening to fling her stuffed elephant at Chrissy. "You are the world's biggest pest, and I don't know what I did to get stuck with you!"

"Well, I'm dying to find out," Chrissy joked, poking her head back around the door before she ran down the hall to the bathroom.

Chapter 9

It was a perfect fall day. The trees in the park glowed in shades of red and gold, and the leaves on the ground crunched underfoot. Chrissy resisted the temptation to kick them into the air. She always did this at home, scattering the leaves her brother Jimmy was trying to rake into a neat pile. Then Jimmy would chase her with the rake, but she always got away.

If only . . . If only what? Chrissy asked herself. *If only I could tell Hunter the truth.*

She glanced up at him when he wasn't looking. He looked even more handsome than the day before, in a big black-and-white turtleneck sweater and black corduroys. Chrissy wanted to pinch herself to make sure she wasn't dreaming, but just then Hunter touched her elbow lightly, and she knew he was real.

"It's a beautiful day, isn't it?" she stammered.

He smiled at her. "I love the fall in San Francisco," he said. "I think it's my favorite time of year. Lovely warm days, crisp nights, clear skies. Who could ask for anything more?"

"And the best thing is that we don't have to worry about snow coming in a few weeks," Chrissy said without thinking.

"Have you lived in places where it snows in winter?" Hunter asked.

Chrissy realized instantly that she'd talked herself into a trap. "One or two," she said hastily. "I hate cold winters, don't you?"

"I like snow in small doses," Hunter answered. "We go up to our cabin in the mountains every weekend in the winter time to ski, but it's nice to come back here on Sunday night. I wouldn't want to have to dig a path in the snow just to get to the street. That's no fun, I bet."

"I wouldn't like to do that," Chrissy said, thinking of all the times she and Will had been out at dawn, shoveling snow out of the driveway.

"I hope you won't be disappointed in this art fair," Hunter said, putting his hand out. He took hold of Chrissy's dangling sleeve, obviously thinking he'd found her hand. He dropped the sleeve in surprise. "Chrissy, what happened to your hand?"

Chrissy looked down at her sleeve and giggled. "I guess my sleeves are a little too long," she said. "You know, big sweaters are in style this year."

"I'll say," Hunter said, grinning at the enormous pullover. "Did you get that in England? I hear they're very popular there—to hide all those bulges from too much fish and chips."

Remembering the safety pin holding up her pants,

Chrissy asked uncomfortably, "Are you hinting that I'm hiding bulges under this big sweater?"

"Of course not," Hunter said hastily. "You're not too fat. I like well-built girls."

I'm too fat, Chrissy remarked to herself. *The diet starts today.*

Hunter peeled back her sleeve and found her hand hidden inside. "Oh, here it is," he said delightedly, and entwined her fingers with his. Chrissy felt as if a current of electricity had zipped all the way up her arm. Hunter, however, seemed unaffected as he continued walking.

"I was saying," he went on, "that I hope you're not bored by this art show. It's just local artists in the park. I'm afraid after Europe you won't find much in the way of adventurous art in San Francisco. Most of it is rather conventional."

Hunter led Chrissy through a gap in a high hedge to a grassy area bordered by shrubs, now dotted with easels and stalls displaying all kinds of artwork. "Well, here we are," Hunter said.

Chrissy glanced around the fair and decided that the art looked similar to the stuff they had unloaded at school—lots of paintings of splotches and streaks, some crooked pots, ceramic wind chimes, and fabric creations. Quickly she went through Caroline's instructions in her head: *Creative if I don't understand it and interesting if I hate it.*

They paused to look at a display of entirely black paintings. To Chrissy the paintings looked as if the artist had just wanted to use up an extra can of black spray paint, but Hunter remarked, "You can sense the rage, can't you?"

Chrissy agreed, and they walked on. A few easels down a painting of a mountain scene caught her eye. Chrissy thought it was so realistic she could almost hear a tumbling waterfall. "Oh, look at that," she blurted out. "Isn't that—"

"Yes, isn't it primitive?" Hunter said with a chuckle. "It's like something a kid would paint. I can't believe anyone would have the nerve to show it."

Chrissy swallowed back her comments in disappointment. How could she be so wrong about art? Hunter obviously knew a lot, and he thought it was terrible— did that mean she was a bad judge of art? *I guess I've got a lot to learn*, she thought. *I'd better watch what I say more carefully. I don't want him to guess how ignorant I am.*

They walked on farther. Chrissy called a sculpture made of thin metal rods "creative" and Hunter agreed with her. As they wandered about the fair discussing the exhibits, she listened carefully to what Hunter had to say. She began to feel more confident, and contributed more comments from Caroline's repertoire. She said certain pieces were "creative" and was delighted when Hunter agreed with her. She even called one or two things "interesting," and Hunter agreed with that, too, although she didn't think he meant the same thing she did.

Finally they paused beside a large exhibit of multimedia creations—wood and metal and fabric all stuck together. A high stool had been placed in the middle, and on the seat sat a plate containing a chicken sandwich with a fork stuck in it. Chrissy wanted to say it was funny, but knew enough now to keep her real opinions to herself. "Oh, look at that," she said, examining the chicken sandwich sculpture. "Isn't that interesting? I'm sure the artist has something important to say, the way he pierced the sandwich with the fork like that." She moved forward to touch it.

"Hey, leave that alone," a bearded middle-aged man yelled, darting out from behind the stall. "That's my lunch!"

Chrissy and Hunter looked at each other. For a second their eyes met in complete understanding, and they burst out laughing.

"That's enough art for one day," Hunter said, squeezing her hand. "Why don't we go get some lunch, too? I have to show up back at the house in time to get ready for one of my parents' parties this evening, so we haven't got too long. What do you feel like eating?"

"Anything you like," Chrissy said, relaxing for the first time that day, now that she and Hunter had finally had an honest laugh together. "I like any kind of food. You choose."

"There's a good sushi restaurant nearby," Hunter said. "How do you feel about that?"

"Fine," she said, wondering what sushi was. She had eaten Chinese food a few times with Caroline's family. Surely Japanese food couldn't be too different?

Hunter led her into a stark white room and seated her on the bar stool next to him. A huge turntable slowly revolved behind the glass counter. In the middle of the turntable was an open area where the Japanese chef waved a sharp knife in one hand. Chrissy peered over the turntable. It was filled with a beautiful array of bite-size morsels, some green and white in squares, others slim and pink, and still others round and wrapped in green.

"Any preference, or do you want me to order?" Hunter asked.

"You go ahead, anything is fine with me," Chrissy said gratefully. Hunter pointed to various objects as they came past, and the chef lifted them skillfully onto the plates. Chrissy looked down with interest as the chef placed the dish in front of her. She had expected Japanese food to consist of bowls of steaming rice with platters of spicy cooked meats, like the Chinese food she'd tasted. In fact, she was hungry, and the small bits in front of her did not look as if they would fill up even half her empty stomach.

"I think a light lunch is a good idea, don't you?" Hunter asked. "Especially for me, I mean. I'll probably make a pig of myself at the party tonight."

He picked up his fork and stabbed a skinny pink strip. Chrissy copied him. She put the stuff into her mouth and chewed. It was a strange taste—cold and wet and slimy.

"What do you think of the sushi?" Hunter asked.

"It takes like raw fish!" Chrissy answered, smiling as if she was enjoying eating it.

To her surprise Hunter threw back his head and laughed. "You have a terrific sense of humor," he said. "Your one-liners are so dry! Tastes like raw fish . . . that's really funny."

What did I say? Chrissy wondered. She didn't dare comment on any of the food for the rest of the meal, although she discovered some strange new flavors and textures. Chrissy decided she would avoid sushi in the future.

I hope Caroline can hurry up with her crash course, she thought desperately. *It seems like there is so much I don't know about living in the city. Hunter has been brought up in a completely different world—it's like being dropped on another planet.* It crossed Chrissy's mind that this was a dumb way to live, but every time she glanced across at Hunter, his warm, brown eyes lit up as he smiled, and she decided that it was worth it to be with him.

Chapter 10

"How did it go?" Caroline asked the moment Chrissy arrived home later that afternoon. "Did you survive the art fair?"

"The art fair wasn't too bad," Chrissy admitted. "Your advice worked pretty well. A couple of times I said something was creative because I didn't understand it. And Hunter would say, 'Yes, it's very creative, isn't it!' So I didn't stick my foot in it too badly at the art fair, except that I thought somebody's lunch was a modern sculpture."

Caroline giggled. "You did what?"

Chrissy giggled, too. "Well, how was I to know that a sandwich with a fork stuck in it was a real lunch? People make sculptures out of the weirdest things!"

"What did Hunter say about that?"

"He thought it was very funny. We both laughed all the way to the restaurant."

"So you had a wonderful time with Hunter again, and he still thinks you're terrific?" Caroline asked.

"He seems to," Chrissy said hesitantly. "He thinks I'm very funny. Only half the time I make jokes that I don't even know I'm making, Caroline. Like lunch today. We went to this place called Sushi and I ate this long pink thing and it was all disgusting and slimy. I said it tasted like raw fish, because it did, and Hunter burst out laughing and said I had a dry sense of humor. What did I say?" Chrissy asked her cousin, but Caroline was laughing too hard to answer.

"Oh, not you, too," Chrissy said in despair. "Do you know how exasperating it is to say something serious and everyone laughs?"

"I'm sorry," Caroline said, smiling. "But it was rather funny. You see, Chrissy—you *were* eating raw fish!"

"I ate what?" Chrissy exclaimed.

Caroline nodded. "That little pink strip was probably a bit of raw tuna or salmon."

"Raw fish?" Chrissy turned up her nose in disgust. "Yuck! No wonder it tasted so weird. And what was that green stuff? That wasn't fish, too, was it?"

"That was seaweed."

"Seaweed?" Chrissy squeaked. "I was eating raw fish and seaweed? What does the guy think I am—a mermaid?"

Caroline laughed again. "It's very fashionable to eat sushi," she said, "and it is excellent for a diet. Which reminds me, while you were gazing into Hunter's eyes, I was slaving over your diet sheet. I've now planned a whole list of foods you can eat and food you can't eat for every meal. Come into the bedroom and I'll show you."

Chrissy followed her cousin obediently and took the paper that Caroline handed her. "Breakfast: one half grapefruit, granola with non-fat milk," she read. Her eye skimmed down the page: no sugar, no peanut butter, no pancakes, no spaghetti, no baked potatoes with sour cream or butter, no candy bars . . . "This is torture," Chrissy said. "You've cut out all the things I love most."

"I know," Caroline agreed. "But it's the only way if you really want to lose weight. When you get down to the weight you want to be, you can start adding a little sugar."

"But I can't eat cereal without sugar!" Chrissy groaned, "and I sure as anything can't eat grapefruit without sugar. Holy cow! I mean, mon dieu! If Hunter weren't such a total babe, I'd never go through with this."

"And you need some exercise to go with it," Caroline advised. "You should jog before school, maybe."

Chrissy's bright blue eyes opened very wide. "You want me to eat nothing except rabbit food and then run up and down these hills in San Francisco?" she asked. "Are you crazy?"

"I don't want anything," Caroline said smoothly. "I thought you were the one who wanted to lose some weight. I'm just offering my expert advice. If you don't want to do it, fine. I'm sure Hunter will still like you when you turn into a blimp."

"I am not turning into a blimp, Caroline Kirby," Chrissy said angrily.

"Not yet," Caroline said, "but I've been thinking about this, Chrissy. If you've put on five pounds in two months here and you're planning to stay nearly a year, you could be thirty pounds heavier by the time you go home—and that would be a blimp! What would Ben say if he came to meet you at the airport and you waddled out of the plane?"

"I guess you're right," Chrissy said quickly. She'd been taken off guard by Caroline's mention of Ben, and she felt a pang of guilt which she pushed to the back of her mind. She preferred to think about Hunter today. "And maybe Hunter does think I should lose a little weight. He made a joke about my big sweater today. That might be his way of telling me nicely that I'm too fat." She looked at the diet sheet, sighed, and put it down again. "Okay. I'd better go through with this, I suppose. Just think—no pizza, no cheeseburgers and fries, no apple pies and chocolate chip cookies. I hope Hunter is worth all this. I don't know if I'll survive the next couple of weeks."

"Give yourself a goal," Caroline said. "Decide that you're going to lose five pounds in time for the Carnival in Venice dance. Then you can choose a really slinky costume for the ball and everyone will be envious!"

"If I don't keep fainting from hunger," Chrissy said, giving Caroline a long, sad face. "Or I don't slip down the bathtub drain first."

Caroline giggled as she left Chrissy to study her diet sheet.

* * *

The next morning Chrissy woke up with a horrible gnawing feeling in her stomach. She lay in bed wondering if she might be sick, until she realized she was incredibly hungry. The night before all she'd eaten was one slice of lean beef, a pile of green beans, and a pear. Now she felt as if she'd been lost in the desert without food for at least a month. Visions of pancakes dripping with syrup, fried eggs with great mounds of hash browns, and strips of crisp bacon danced in front of her eyes. She staggered up and walked through to the kitchen.

To Chrissy's surprise, Caroline was already there. "Here's your breakfast," she said, pointing to a bowl with about a half inch of granola in it, and some banana slices on top. "I thought I'd prepare it for you so that you weren't tempted."

"Thanks a lot," Chrissy said dryly. She sat and looked at the granola. "I bet you're enjoying this, aren't you?" she asked Caroline as she poured on the non-fat milk. "I bet you're getting a kick out of watching someone else suffer while you can eat."

"You have to want to do this, Chrissy," Caroline said. "I'm not forcing you to do anything. I'm only trying to help."

Chrissy managed a smile. "I know you are. Sorry I'm being such an old grouch. I feel like a horse kicked me in the stomach. In fact, if I came face to face with a horse, he'd better watch out, because I might eat him."

Caroline laughed and got up to fix her lunch.

"So what am I allowed for lunch?" Chrissy asked. "I

don't have my diet sheet with me, but I suppose it's probably one lettuce leaf and one celery stick."

"Not as bad as that," Caroline consoled, slipping her own sandwich into a bag. "You can have *two* celery sticks, and some carrot sticks, too, if you're very good."

"I'll never make it through the day," Chrissy said. "I'll pass out in choir and an ambulance will have to take me home."

"Don't make such a big deal of this, Chrissy," Caroline said. "Girls at school go on diets all the time. The first couple of days will be the worst, because you'll still be hungry. Just stick with it and you'll be glad. I'll make some yogurt dip to go with your carrot sticks, okay?" she offered.

Chrissy looked up and smiled. "Thanks, Caroline," she said. "You're a nice person, you know that?"

"Thanks, Chrissy," Caroline said, looking pleased.

"And since you're such a nice person," Chrissy went on hurriedly, "I wondered whether you'd lend me your black sweater today, just in case I meet Hunter around school."

"I suppose so," Caroline said with an exaggerated sigh. "Boy, I'm glad I haven't had to put up with a sister for sixteen years. Two months are bad enough." She walked ahead of Chrissy to the bedroom.

Chrissy scooped up the rest of her granola without enthusiasm. *Why does diet food have to taste boring?* she wondered. *Maybe when I leave school I'll invent a kind of diet food that tastes rich and sinful, and I'll make a million!*

Chrissy felt much better by the time she went to

school, making plans in her head for diet double-chocolate cakes and diet hot fudge sundaes.

But the day at school seemed to go on forever. All Chrissy could think about was food. She had to stop herself from eating her lunch during the morning break. To make things worse, she didn't catch one glimpse of Hunter all day. In fact, she felt as if everything that happened that day had been planned to make dieting as difficult as possible. Every song in choir class suddenly involved food. They started with "If Music Be the Food of Love," and went on to "Chestnuts Roasting on an Open Fire." After that Chrissy couldn't get her mind off food no matter how hard she tried. When they sang "My Melancholy Baby," all she could think of were sweet honeydew melons, pink watermelons, and cauliflower dripping with cheese sauce.

In English they were reading a story by Stephen Crane about four men at sea.

"Will you read now, Chrissy?" Mrs. Doyle asked.

Chrissy looked down at her book and began to read: "'Finally he spoke. "Billie," he murmured dreamfully, "what kind of pie do you like best?"'"

"Go on, Chrissy," Mrs. Doyle prodded when Chrissy abruptly stopped reading. Chrissy stared down at the page, but said nothing. "Is there a problem?" her teacher said.

Chrissy forced herself to continue reading. She could hardly tell her English teacher that it was torture to read about pies. She tried to shut them out of her mind, but they floated before her eyes for the rest of the class period—thick apple pies with big scoops of ice cream on top, blueberry pies and cherry pies and rich, dark meat pies, all made with her mother's light flaky crust.

When she walked into math class, Chrissy heaved a big sigh of relief. At least she'd be able to concentrate on numbers. What could there possibly be to remind her of food?

"We'll tackle the word problems on page thirty-two," her math teacher said cheerfully. "Numbers two, five, and seven."

Chrissy picked up her pencil and looked at number two: "The number of chickens cooked for a barbecue . . ." it began.

"Aaaahhh!" Chrissy moaned, and slammed her book shut. Twenty pairs of eyes looked up at her with interest. Chrissy blushed and pretended to be busy.

I don't believe this, Chrissy thought. *This is a plot against me!*

"Is something wrong, Chrissy?" her teacher asked.

Yes, I can't stop thinking about food, Chrissy thought. But out loud she said, "I'm just finding number two very difficult, Miss Johnston. Do you think I could skip it and do number three instead?"

"I don't see what's particularly hard about number two," Miss Johnston said earnestly. "But if it's causing you problems, why don't we work through it together. Come up to my desk."

Chrissy reluctantly carried her book up to the teacher's desk.

"No," Miss Johnston began. "The number of chickens cooked for a barbecue is such that every guest can have two helpings. The bigger chickens are cut into quarters, the smaller ones in halves. Have you got that so far, Chrissy? Can you picture it?"

Chrissy pictured it so clearly that Miss Johnston herself was in danger of looking like a chicken. It was a long half hour before they finally finished struggling with the problem and Chrissy was allowed to return to her seat, her stomach rumbling uncomfortably.

I'll never survive, she thought as she closed her eyes. *I'm beginning to wonder whether even Hunter is worth all this!*

Chapter 11

Chrissy woke up around midnight from a troubled sleep. In her dream she had been back home in Danbury. It was Thanksgiving and the whole family was gathered around the table. The crisp white cloth was barely visible beneath the dishes piled on top. Her father stood at the head, carving a huge turkey. The traditional seven sweets and seven sours of the Maddens' German ancestors had been placed around the table along with stuffing and cranberry sauce, muffins and pickles, and lots of other delicious dishes. Chrissy had just held up her plate to be filled when her father looked at her anxiously. "I'm sorry, honey, but you're on a diet," he'd said.

Chrissy lay in silence for a moment while her stomach grumbled and growled.

It's no use, she decided. *I have to eat something.*

She got up, glanced at Caroline's neatly sleeping body, and tiptoed into the kitchen. Blinking in the light of the refrigerator, she let her gaze wander from the cold roast beef to the remains of the potato salad to the block of cheese. She opened the freezer and spied a carton of ice cream hiding in the back. *How can I say no to mint chocolate chip?* she asked herself, then grabbed the ice cream and carried it across to the table.

"Caught in the act!" came a voice behind her. She spun around and saw Caroline standing in the doorway. "I thought I heard noises in the kitchen," she said. "Your diet sure didn't last long, did it?"

"I couldn't help it, Cara. I was starving. I dreamed about Thanksgiving and they wouldn't let me have any turkey," Chrissy pleaded.

"But the first night, Chrissy! You might at least have held out for a couple of days! Where's your willpower?"

"It's all right for you!" Chrissy snapped, angry because Caroline had made her feel guilty. "You're lucky. Look how skinny you are. I bet you never needed to diet. You can't imagine what agony I've been going through."

"I can imagine pretty well," Caroline said. "Because you've done nothing but talk about it every minute since you started this diet. You told me how you'd suffered last night during breakfast. You told me how you'd suffered all day at school while I was changing for ballet. Frankly, Chrissy, I'm finding your dieting and suffering a little boring!"

Chrissy opened her mouth but no words came out. Caroline was usually a peaceful person, so when she got mad, Chrissy knew she'd done something wrong.

"I don't know why I bothered to help you," Caroline went on. "I thought the whole idea was crazy from the beginning. I thought it could never work, trying to turn yourself into somebody you're not, but I went along with it because I could see that it meant a lot to you. I gave up my spare time, of which I have even less than usual these days, to write lists of artists and art galleries and to plan a complete diet for you. And now you blow the diet after the first full day! Next time I won't bother."

Chrissy could feel her cheeks flushing with embarrassment. At home she would have gotten into a shouting match with one of her brothers if he'd criticized her like that, but somehow it was very hard to yell at Caroline. Chrissy also had a sneaking feeling that Caroline was right. She'd been wallowing in self-pity, talking about nothing but her diet, when all the time Caroline was only trying to help her.

"Gee, I'm sorry, Cara," she muttered. "You're right, I've been really selfish."

Caroline's scowl slowly turned into a smile. "It's okay. I think it's called having withdrawal symptoms. You're withdrawing from food!"

"That's what it feels like," Chrissy said. "I know I've gone on and on about it, but I don't think you can understand how hard it is for me. Your family doesn't make a big deal about eating. With my family it's different. Meals are the big event of the day. We have piles and piles of food, and we all sit and relax around the table. Everyone looks forward to mealtime."

Caroline smiled and nodded. "I understand," she said.

Chrissy opened the freezer and put back the ice

cream. "Cutting out food is cutting out an important part of my life," she said.

"You don't have to stick to the diet if you don't want to, Chrissy," Caroline said. "Nobody is making you."

"But I don't want to turn into a blimp," Chrissy replied.

"So you have to make a decision," Caroline said. "Do you want to lose weight more than you want to eat?"

"I guess I do," Chrissy said. "I want Hunter to like me." She grinned. "And I want to be able to wear your clothes. Maybe we could rewrite the diet with just a bit more food . . ."

"I guess we could do that," Caroline said. "And I tell you what—I'll go on the diet with you, if you think it would help."

Chrissy looked at Caroline with amazement. "You don't have to do that for me, Cara. You certainly don't need to diet. You're perfect just the way you are."

"I'm not so sure about that," Caroline said hesitantly. "You see, I might be a bit heavy for a dancer."

"That's baloney," Chrissy said. "I saw you on stage, remember? You looked perfect."

"For a chorus line, maybe," Caroline said. She perched herself on the edge of the kitchen table and began playing with the edge of the table mat. "But if I ever wanted to dance a duet . . ."

"What difference would that make?"

"The boy would have to lift me," Caroline said. She stared at the table mat in silence, and continued fiddling with it. Chrissy sensed the tension in Caroline's movement.

"And you think you're too heavy for a boy to lift you?" Chrissy asked quietly. "Is that what's bugging you?"

"Uh-huh," Caroline said, still not looking up. Then she took a deep breath. "Chrissy, do you remember when I came home all excited about the art fair and you asked me if I'd been asked to dance with Baryshnikov?"

Chrissy grinned, "And you said you wished!"

At last Caroline looked up, her eyes glowing. "Well, strangely enough, it's almost come true."

"Oh, Caroline, surely Baryshnikov would be able to lift you," Chrissy said, bewildered.

Caroline giggled. "No, another great male dancer. There's this boy who's just joined our dance school, Chrissy. His name is Carl, and he's the most fantastic dancer I've ever seen. And he looks, well, like a Greek god!"

"Do I get the feeling that it's not just his dancing that interests you?" Chrissy asked her cousin.

"I don't know yet," Caroline said. "I know I can't stop looking at him in class, and every time he comes near me, I get goose bumps up and down my spine. You remember when you asked me if Alex gives me goose bumps?"

"I remember."

Caroline's cheeks turned rosy pink. "Well, this guy does."

"So what do you plan to do about it?" Chrissy asked.

"I don't know. Right now he doesn't even know my name. I'm just one of the girls in the class. He doesn't treat me any differently from anyone else—in fact, he's a bit reserved. He hardly talks to anyone unless it concerns ballet class."

"So you think you have to dance with him to get to know him better?" Chrissy said.

"That's just it," Caroline answered, looking up excitedly. "Tonight Madame announced that two dancers from our school will have the honor of performing a duet in an opera—a real opera! It's pretty obvious that Carl will be the guy. Did I mention his name was Carl, by the way? That's a nice name, don't you think?"

"And you'd like to be the girl?" guessed Chrissy.

Caroline gave a dreamy sigh. "Imagine dancing a duet with Carl—being lifted up in his arms! He'd have to notice me then, wouldn't he?"

"I guess he would," Chrissy agreed.

"Which is why I'd better lose some weight, Chrissy," Caroline insisted. "There's this girl named Tais, you see. She's got the best chance. She has wrists this big"—Caroline formed a tiny circle with her thumb and finger—"and she's like a little china doll. So I thought if I could lose enough weight, maybe I'd stand a chance."

Chrissy eyed her cousin critically. "I still don't think you need to lose weight, Cara. Where would you lose it from? You don't have an ounce of flab on you."

"My thighs are a little heavy," Caroline admitted.

"That's from all that dancing. I bet all dancers have heavy thighs," Chrissy said.

"Not Tais. Tais has thighs like little deer's legs—all spindly. When she leaps, she seems to hang in the air, as if she weighed nothing at all." Caroline leaned forward earnestly. "She's really good, Chrissy. In fact, she's super good."

"But you're good, too, Cara. You were the best one in that dance I went to," Chrissy said warmly.

Caroline shook her head. "I'm okay," she said. "But the only way I can compete with her is to lose weight, Chrissy. So tomorrow I'll write out a diet sheet for both of us. Then you can get Hunter and I'll get Carl and we'll both live happily ever after."

"What about poor Alex?" Chrissy asked. "You can't just dump him. He's so nice."

"I know," Caroline said hesitantly. "And I don't really want to dump him, any more than you want to dump Ben. I just feel the way you do—that someone as exciting as Carl might only happen to me once in my life, and I don't want to miss my one chance."

Chrissy nodded in understanding. "Maybe we're both crazy," she said. "I'm chasing after a boy who will probably be voted Most Sophisticated at Maxwell High, and you're chasing after a temperamental ballet dancer, when we both have nice, steady boyfriends who would do anything for us."

"Do you really think we're crazy?" Caroline asked, looking at her cousin seriously.

Chrissy considered the possibilities, then grinned mischievously. "Nah, we just want to live a little before we get old. I say let's go for it!"

Chapter 12

For the rest of that week Chrissy felt as if she were living in a daze. This feeling was partly caused by her diet, which made her feel light-headed and weak. She wouldn't have been surprised if the strong autumn winds off the bay swept her away.

The other reason for her strange mood was Hunter. He seemed to be growing more interested in her every day. He showed up unexpectedly at lunch on Wednesday to whisk her away from school to a fashionable restaurant. Every day they went over to the old gym together after school to finish setting up the exhibition for Saturday's judging and grand opening. Already physically exhausted from lack of food, Chrissy found being with Hunter mentally exhausting. She always had such a good time when she was with him, that she had to keep reminding herself to watch what she said so she wouldn't give away her secret.

If only Hunter were not the son of a rich, artistic

family . . . if only he'd been brought up to the sort of casual life Chrissy was used to . . . if only he knew the truth about her, and she didn't have to keep pretending . . . if only she had the nerve to set him straight about who she was. *We would have such a great time together, if only his background and mine weren't so different,* she thought. *After all, he is funny, and he knows how to enjoy life. But the things he likes are so different from the things I like. I can't go on feeling like a fish out of water. If only I didn't feel this way about him . . .*

The trouble was that every time Chrissy was with Hunter, she felt as if she were acting a part. She could never relax and laugh freely, the way she could with her friends at home—like Ben. Whenever she thought of Ben, she felt guilty. But she hadn't received a letter from him in a few weeks, and she was thinking about him less as she thought more about Hunter.

Chrissy knew that Caroline was experiencing a similar situation with Alex and Carl. She saw less of Alex because she was putting in extra ballet practice to be with Carl. Caroline even missed setting up for the art fair. Chrissy rarely saw her cousin until they both collapsed into bed at night.

"Look at us," Caroline said on Thursday night, propping herself up on her elbow and giggling at her cousin. "We look like we've just come home from a battle. Is this how you imagined love would be, Chrissy?"

Chrissy lifted her head up and giggled, too. "I never thought it would be such hard work," she confessed.

"Me neither."

"So how is your campaign going?" Chrissy asked.

'Has Carl noticed yet that you're the only girl in the class worth looking at?"

Caroline sighed. "I don't think so, but I did get to demonstrate something with him tonight. Madame asked us to show the supported arabesque."

"That's great—whatever that is," Chrissy said with enthusiasm.

"The boy holds the girl by her arms and turns her around while she has one leg in the air behind her back," Caroline explained.

"Sounds complicated," Chrissy remarked.

"Not really. I got to hold Carl's hands for ten minutes, though," said Caroline with a smile.

"It's a start."

"Yeah, but Tais got to demonstrate a lift with him. That's when the boy puts his hand on the girl's waist and sets her on his shoulder. Imagine! If looks could have killed, she'd be lying pretty still by now."

Chrissy laughed. "And I thought you were a sweet and gentle thing when I first met you."

"You have no idea what dark thoughts go through my mind!" Caroline said, grinning. Then she gave another sigh. "Oh, well, I'd better get moving with that diet. I haven't even lost one pound yet. That scale in the bathroom has got to be wrong. All I ate all day were celery sticks and a carton of yogurt."

"That's not enough, Cara," Chrissy said, suddenly serious. "You can't dance all evening on that little bit of food. You'll get sick."

"I'll be fine," Caroline said. "I've got to get down to Tais's weight fast, Chrissy."

"Don't overdo this, Cara, okay?" Chrissy asked.

"Don't worry about me," Caroline reassured her "How did your day go? Did you keep to the diet al day?"

"I'm very proud of myself," Chrissy said. "Justin was handing around brownies at lunchtime and I turned her down. And you know how I love chocolate brownies."

"Good for you, Chrissy. I can see the difference in you already."

"You can?" Chrissy asked, pleased.

"Sure," Caroline answered. "Those jeans don't look as if they're about to split anymore."

"I thought they felt more comfortable today. Hey that's great. It's nice to know I'm suffering for a good cause."

"And I take it you saw Hunter after school?"

Chrissy gave a broad grin. "We worked for a while on the banners in the gym and then we went to a foreign film festival."

"How was it?" Caroline asked.

Chrissy wrinkled her nose. "I'm not sure," she said "I couldn't understand a word they were saying."

"Didn't they have subtitles?"

"Oh, sure, but they didn't seem to make sense either We saw two movies—one was from Poland and had these two guys sitting on a deserted railway station for an hour. After half an hour one of them went to get a bicycle, and in the end they laughed and took out sandwiches and ate them. That was the whole thing, Cara." Chrissy threw her hands up in exasperation. "The other movie was Japanese. It had these people kneeling on the floor crying for an hour while birds flew past an oper window. When the people weren't crying they said things like, 'The cranes have to come back,' but I never understood why anyone was crying. In fact, I never understood a thing!"

Caroline chuckled. "Poor Chrissy. Did Hunter like them?"

"He said they made an important statement." Chrissy shrugged her shoulders. "The one good thing about the evening was that I fell asleep in the Japanese one and woke up with my head on his shoulder. That was nice."

Caroline grinned. "When your folks sent you to San Francisco to get a dose of culture, I bet they never dreamed it would be this much," she said.

"I don't know about my parents, but *I* certainly never dreamed it would be this much," Chrissy agreed. "I didn't know this much culture existed. I just wonder how long I can keep this up, Cara."

Chrissy had wondered the same thing more than once that week, then on Friday she found herself even more confused. She was hurrying down the hall toward choir class when she bumped into Marvin Jones—the huge football star she'd met when she had first started school at Maxwell. She ran around the corner and found the passage blocked by Marvin's huge bulk. She bounced off him as if he were a trampoline, her books falling from her hands.

"Gee, I'm sorry," she mumbled, before she looked up to see Marvin's familiar, grinning face.

"The way you go charging into people, I should use you as one of my linebackers," he said. "Here . . ." He bent with surprising agility to pick up her books for her.

"Thanks." Chrissy grinned. "I hope I didn't hur
you."

Marvin threw back his head and laughed heartily. "I
would take a lot more than just a little girl like you t
hurt big old Marvin here," he said.

Chrissy giggled. "I'd better be heading for choir," sh
said.

"And I've got to get over to the locker room to tall
things over with the coach," Marvin said. "Big gam
tonight. You going to come and watch?"

"Um . . . I'm not sure," Chrissy replied.

"I haven't seen you at a game in a long time," Mar
vin said. "It's kind of quiet without Chrissy Madde
cheering us on! You have to come tonight and watch u
win back the Bell."

"The Bell?"

"It's a special trophy that was started between us an
Lincoln High almost a hundred years ago. You see, on
year some guys from Maxwell stole the bell from th
tower at Lincoln High after beating them in a footbal
game. Then the next year, Maxwell challenged Lincol
to win the bell back, and it's been a tradition eve
since."

"Gee, that's really a neat story," Chrissy remarked.

"Well, Lincoln has held it for four years now, but w
aim to get it back tonight, so we need all the cheering
we can get."

"It sounds like it will be a great game," Chrissy said.

"I'll be watching for you," Marvin replied, waving
his huge hand as he turned to go. "Only don't you g
yelling at me if I drop the ball, okay?"

Chrissy was smiling as she hurried on to choir. *A big

football game and Marvin asked me specially to be there!
she thought excitedly. Back home she never missed a
football game. They were the highlight of the week, not
only for Chrissy, but for the entire town of Danbury.
She could imagine it clearly—the band in their bright
uniforms, herself and the rest of the cheerleaders yelling
loudly and kicking their heels up, the ball sailing through
the air, the Danbury Hornets racing down the field, one
player breaking through the line of defense and running
for the end zone, catching the ball with a flying leap,
and the stadium erupting in wild cheers. Marvin's right,
she thought. *I haven't been to a game in ages, and I
really miss that excitement.*

After school Chrissy found Hunter was waiting for
her in the student parking lot. He was leaning against
the white Porsche, his arms folded across his chest. He
gave her a quick kiss and squeezed her hand, then
opened the door for her and they drove away. As usual
Chrissy felt the need to pinch herself to make sure this
was really happening. Never in her wildest dreams had
she envisioned herself running out of the school straight
into the arms of a gorgeous guy such as Hunter, then
being driven off in his white sports car while everyone
else looked on with envy.

She leaned back in the seat and sighed.

"Tired?" he asked.

She nodded. "End of the week tired."

"Too tired to go out tonight?"

"Oh, no. I always get my second wind by evening.
There's a big football game on tonight—did you
know?"

"Oh, sure—the Bell game. Rah! Rah!" Hunter

said sarcastically. "All these old men stagger out to watch the game and renew the old rivalry."

Chrissy didn't say anything.

"Dumb, huh?" Hunter asked.

"I guess so," she answered, but inside she was disappointed.

"And the old men get dressed up in their old Maxwell football shirts and blow horns and things."

"Sounds stupid," Chrissy said, silently apologizing to Marvin.

"And if you dare sit near them," Hunter went on, "they give you the entire history of every Bell game they've ever watched."

Chrissy raised her eyes in a sign of boredom. Hunter nodded as if he understood. "So I take it you're not wild about being crammed in the bleachers with three thousand other people tonight?" he asked. "I get the feeling you think football is a pretty stupid waste of time, right?"

Chrissy hesitated. She felt as if she were betraying Marvin and the rest of the Maxwell team as well as the Danbury Hornets, but she couldn't admit to Hunter that there wasn't much she enjoyed more than a good football game. "Er, right," she agreed at last.

"So that's settled," Hunter said with a sigh. "We'll skip the game and do something more intellectual, right?"

"Right," Chrissy said, trying to sound enthusiastic.

"I know something you might like," Hunter said brightly. "My dad has a couple of tickets to a really avant-garde concert you might enjoy. It should be interesting." He paused and looked across at her. "You would rather go to the concert than the football game, wouldn't you?"

"Oh, sure," Chrissy heard herself saying, "I'd much rather go to the concert."

But that evening she regretted those words bitterly. The concert was by a modern Finnish composer and consisted of a concerto for a flute, a few garbage cans, and two vacuum cleaners. At first Chrissy wondered if it was meant to be funny. She certainly thought the man in a tuxedo banging two garbage-can lids together was pretty amusing. But nobody else in the audience was smiling. They didn't even smile when another man turned the page in his score and switched on one of the vacuum cleaners. In fact, everyone around Chrissy seemed to be lost in concentration. She couldn't understand how anyone could call this horrible racket "music."

The concerto went on and on. It had been bad enough with just the noise of the garbage cans and the vacuum cleaners, but when a woman in black started to attack her flute, Chrissy thought her eardrums would burst. The woman's fingers flew up and down the keys, producing notes that reminded Chrissy of the sounds that came from the farm next door around hog-slaughtering time.

I could be watching Marvin beat the pants off Lincoln, she thought. *Darn! I can't believe I turned down a football game for this.* She glanced across at Hunter. *I really like him,* she thought miserably, *but I'll never learn to like the things he likes, as long as I live!*

Chapter 13

"I only wish I knew what to do," Caroline said for the twentieth time on Saturday.

"Of course you should go to the extra ballet rehearsal," Chrissy insisted. "They can do without you at the art fair for one morning."

"But the whole committee is supposed to be there for the grand opening after the judging," Caroline said. "I don't want the others to think I'm avoiding my responsibilities."

"I'll tell you what," Chrissy said. "I'll be happy to go in your place. Hunter asked me before if I could come along, but it was supposed to be committee members only." Chrissy noticed the doubt in Caroline's face. She went on hastily, "That way I can hand around food and help out, but I won't say anything, okay?"

Caroline smiled at her cousin. "You are sweet sometimes," she said. "That would be great, Chrissy. I really appreciate it."

"Stop worrying," Chrissy said. "Put your mind completely on your dancing. Tell yourself you're going to float in the air like a butterfly—and whip that girl Tais's behind while you're at it."

Caroline actually laughed. "That sounds difficult to carry out," she said. "But I will try my best. Madame might select the dancers for the opera today. You never know with her—she's temperamental, like Carl!"

"You can do it, Cara," Chrissy said. "And I'll go stand at the art fair with a stupid grin on my face while people talk to me about art."

"By the way, did you have a good time with Hunter last night?" Caroline asked, cutting a grapefruit in half and placing half in front of Chrissy.

"Oh, fine," Chrissy said. "The music wasn't exactly my kind of stuff, but the ride home was great."

"Alex called this morning," Caroline said. "We won the Bell game, apparently. He said it was so exciting. Everyone was there—the bleachers were packed—and we won the game with a fifty-five yard pass in the last ten seconds. Imagine! I wish I could have gone."

"Me, too," Chrissy said dreamily.

"You could have," Caroline pointed out.

Chrissy looked down at her grapefruit. "Hunter doesn't like football," she murmured.

Caroline grinned. "No, he wouldn't. It's too conventional for him. He makes a point of not liking things other people like."

"That's true," Chrissy said. "He doesn't seem to like anything I like."

Caroline looked at Chrissy with interest. "Do I detect that you're getting fed up with Hunter?"

Chrissy put her spoon down with a clatter on the china plate. "I don't know, Caroline. I really don't know. He's so wonderful in some ways. I feel proud when I'm with him and the other girls look at us." She paused. "I still nearly melt each time he looks at me, and when he kisses me—wow! But you have to have something in common for a relationship to work, don't you? More than kissing, I mean."

"I guess you do," Caroline said.

"I'm trying so hard," Chrissy went on. "I want our relationship to work, and I'm trying to like all the things he likes, but it's so hard for me."

Caroline looked at her steadily. "Maybe you weren't meant to be a culture vulture," she said. "Maybe it's time to admit that Hunter is just not right for you."

Chrissy looked at her cousin, horrified. "Don't say that," she said. "I want him to be right for me. I couldn't bear to give him up. You'll just have to cram in more lessons so I can appreciate foreign films and weird music. Maybe I'm just super slow. Everyone else seemed fascinated with the music and the films. Why does life have to be so difficult?" She dug her spoon savagely into her grapefruit. "Why do all the good foods have to be fattening? And why does grapefruit always have to shoot straight into my eye?"

Caroline started laughing, and Chrissy had to join her.

"All this suffering has got to be worth it in the end, hasn't it, Cara?" Chrissy asked.

"I hope so," Caroline said. "For my sake as well as yours. Here, do you want your slice of diet bread? I'd better get going so that I can warm up properly."

As Caroline hurried out of the room, Chrissy realized that she hadn't eaten anything except her grapefruit. *Cara's gone too far with this diet*, she thought worriedly. *She can't just stop eating.*

She thought about Caroline while she got dressed for the art fair. She knew how hard it must be for her cousin to feel torn between friends and Alex and her life at ballet school. *I'm glad I'm not talented*, she decided. *This way I never have to decide whether to stay ordinary or not. I am ordinary and I'm stuck with it.*

Chrissy arrived at the doorway of the old gym later that morning and peeped inside. The room was full of distinguished-looking people wandering among the exhibits with glasses in their hands, or talking earnestly in groups. She recognized several teachers, including Mr. Yamagata, as well as several committee members. Dominic looked uncomfortable in a conservative suit, while Rainbow was in something that didn't look like it had come from India, and Sacha looked stunning as always in a long black dress. But she couldn't find Hunter, and she hesitated in the doorway, suddenly scared to go further.

Will the others think I don't belong here? Chrissy wondered. She hoped she would have a chance to explain that she was only helping out for Caroline before anyone made a fuss. Then she caught a glimpse of her aunt across the room, talking to two bearded men. The sight of a familiar figure reassured her, and she went in.

What's wrong with me? she wondered as she slinked past the pillars in her aunt's direction. *I never used to be afraid of meeting new people. I didn't think I was scared of anything, and now I feel sick to my stomach every time I have to face people like this. I hate watching every word I say and wondering when someone will catch me in a lie. I really don't belong here, let's face it. I was never shy at football games at home, in front of hundreds of people. Maybe I'd better accept the fact that Hunter is not the right boy for me.*

Her aunt looked up as Chrissy appeared around the last pillar. "Oh, Chrissy dear, how nice to see you," she said. "I guess Caroline decided to go to her dance practice. When I left home earlier this morning she still couldn't make up her mind if she should come here or go to that rehearsal." Aunt Edith paused, and Chrissy thought she caught her aunt smile mysteriously. "Well, I am glad you've become so interested in art, Chrissy. Come over and meet two of the other judges. This is Chrissy Madden, my niece—you know—*City Two Thousand and One*?"

The men beamed at Chrissy. "So it runs in the family, does it?" one man asked.

"It's a good thing we didn't get a chance to see the names earlier or we could be accused of unfair bias," the other man chuckled.

Chrissy looked from one to the other, wondering what they were talking about, but she decided she wasn't sure she wanted to know.

"Well, I'd better go see if I can help pass out the refreshments," she said. "That's what I came for, after all. Caroline didn't want the committee to be short-handed without her."

"A modest little thing," Chrissy heard the first man say as she walked away. Gratefully she slipped through to the kitchen area set up behind the gym and grabbed a plate of stuffed mushrooms. "Do you want me to take this around?" she asked Sacha, who had just come in.

"You don't have to work if you don't want to," Sacha said. "I expect there's a lot of people who want to talk to you."

This gets stranger and stranger every minute, Chrissy thought. *Why would anyone want to talk to me? I'm not even supposed to be here.*

She hurried out with the mushrooms and began handing them around.

"Well, look what I found! It's Cinderella!" Chrissy heard Hunter's voice, deep and mellow, in her ear. He grasped her shoulders gently from behind, then turned her around to face him. "You don't have to be a slave anymore, Cinderella," he said, smiling at her.

"Hunter, what are you talking about?" Chrissy demanded. "Has everyone here gone bananas this morning?"

"You mean you haven't seen yet? You don't even know?" he asked. He took the tray from her hands and put it down firmly on a nearby table. "Come with me, young lady," he said, taking her hand and guiding her across the room.

As they approached the far wall, Chrissy suddenly realized where they were going. She saw her tower of soda cans still standing, but it was now roped off and had an official entry card beside it. "*City Two Thousand and One.* Chrissy Madden, Maxwell High, Junior," was printed on the card, and below the writing a blue rosette saying simply "Most Original."

Chrissy stood gaping at her creation. She couldn't

believe it. The tower of cans still looked like the same tower she'd built, but "*City Two Thousand and One*"?

"Who named it?" she managed to say at last.

Hunter grinned. "I named it for you. I thought it needed a funky name, so I gave it one."

"Oh," was all Chrissy could say.

"I'm so proud of you," Hunter went on excitedly. "I knew when I first saw it that this was the most original thing at the entire fair. I'm glad the judges had the same good taste!"

People began to crowd around them.

"This is Chrissy Madden," Hunter told them. "She's the artist."

Chrissy stood there silently while people shook her hand and said things like "most creative" and "a bold statement." Once she recovered from the shock, she found it difficult to suppress her laughter. *If only they knew that I was only playing around with the trash*, she thought. *I built the tower just for fun, the way my brothers used to do at home. I wonder what they would say if I told them?*

But she knew there was no way she could tell the truth without losing Hunter. He would be furious if she made him look like a fool, that was for sure. Then he'd walk off and she'd never see him again. With this thought in mind, Chrissy kept the false smile on her face and shook more hands.

"That's Edith Kirby's niece," she heard a woman say. "You know—the woman who runs Designs art gallery?"

"Of course," a man agreed. "Interesting how talent

runs in families, isn't it? I wonder if her aunt helped with her creation?"

"Not at all," the woman said in a shocked voice. "That would never do for a judge. I was with Edith Kirby today when we first saw the sculpture. She was truly astonished to find she'd awarded a prize to her niece."

"A very mature approach for a high-schooler," the man commented as they moved off. "Got a great future."

Chrissy was still surprised at the events of the past few minutes, but she no longer thought the situation was so absurd. *Is it possible that I do have talent and I just didn't know it?* she asked herself. *They said that talent runs in families. Maybe I inherited some artistic genes from Aunt Edith. Maybe I really am a great artist!*

Chapter 14

"There, the horse is finished," Chrissy said with satisfaction. "Not bad. Not bad at all. How's that for talent?" Chrissy asked herself out loud.

She leaned back in her seat to eye the painting in front of her. It was a shame that the horse's legs had somehow run into the background, but the bright green of the horse's coat contrasted well with the orange sky and the trees. The trees looked like scrubbing brushes to Chrissy, but reminded her of the trees Hunter had admired so much in a painting at the fair earlier that day. She had to admit that hers was not the sort of painting she would choose to hang on a wall, but it looked to Chrissy just like the paintings everybody had called "bold" and "interesting" at the art fair. And Chrissy enjoyed actually putting the paint on the canvas.

She had just squeezed out a generous length of white to paint clouds when she heard the front door slam.

"Anyone home?" she heard Caroline call. "Yuck. What's that smell?"

"*Buon giorno!*" Chrissy called back.

"Where are you?"

"In the kitchen, creating," Chrissy sang out. She looked up from her work as her cousin came into the kitchen.

"What on earth?" Caroline asked.

Chrissy glanced up at her over the top of the easel. "I've decided to take up painting," she said. "Your mother found some of her old stuff for me. These oils are lots of fun, but they do smell bad."

"So the art fair this morning inspired you, did it?" Caroline asked. "Are you planning to enter the next one?"

"I don't think so," Chrissy said calmly, "since I already won this one."

"You did what?"

"I got a prize for most original."

"Chrissy, you didn't!" Caroline stammered out the words. "But I didn't even know you'd entered. I didn't even know you could paint!"

"I didn't enter a painting. It was a sculpture," Chrissy said, looking back down at her painting and putting in a big blob of fluffy white cloud. "You know —the tower of soda cans?"

"You did that? Chrissy, I don't believe it! Why didn't you tell me before it was yours?"

"I didn't enter it myself—Hunter did," Chrissy answered. "I only built it for fun." She was about to tell Caroline that she had no idea she was creating a sculpture, but her pride wouldn't let her. She experienced a low of warmth at Caroline's expression, and thought again how nice it was to be talented. She was no longer good old Chrissy who tagged along, but Chrissy the creative genius!

"Everyone was saying that I take after your mother," he went on, putting more touches to her painting. They said talent runs in families, so I thought it was about time I made use of mine!"

"Wow, I can't believe you won, Chrissy," Caroline said. "Can I see what you're doing now?"

"Sure," Chrissy replied, painting in another cloud.

Caroline walked around the front of the easel.

"Well?" Chrissy asked, "what do you think of it?"

"Wow," Caroline said again.

"Interesting, isn't it?" Chrissy asked, peppering the orange sky with more clouds as she talked.

"Er, yes, very interesting," Caroline said.

"I want to make a bold statement," Chrissy went on.

"Oh, it's certainly a bold statement," Caroline agreed.

"So you think I was right to paint an orange sky?" Chrissy asked.

"Oh, sure . . . if, er, that's how you see the sky."

"I'm calling it *Day Before Destruction*," Chrissy declared, putting another coat of green on the horse's mane. "You see, the green horse symbolizes the peaceful arms, and the orange in the sky announces a nuclear war. Do you like it?"

Caroline opened her mouth, then shut it again. "It's certainly unusual," she answered.

"You wait until it's finished!" Chrissy said. "I haven't even started using the red yet. Aunt Edith says you have to let one color dry before you can put another one over it."

"Oh, well, I don't want to get in the way," Caroline said. "I'm tired enough to drop, and pretty depressed, too. Did the opening go smoothly without me?"

"It was fine," Chrissy said. "We didn't even notice you weren't there."

"Oh," Caroline replied. Chrissy was concentrating so hard on her painting that she didn't see her cousin's face.

"I don't really know whether painting is my thing," Chrissy went on. "Maybe I'm just a born sculptor."

"I'm beginning to wonder if I'm a born anything," Caroline said wearily. "Certainly not a born dancer like Tais."

"Aunt Edith said she'd see if she had a block of soapstone around the gallery so that I could try it," Chrissy continued. "I'm dying to attack something with a chisel!"

"I'm dying to attack something with a chisel, too," Caroline said. "Or rather, somebody. It all comes so easily to Tais. She can do a move over and over again and never get tired. And her leaps—Chrissy, when she leaps, it's as if she's suspended in air. I know she's going to get the part. I just know it. She got to go through a whole sequence with Carl today."

"Oh, that's too bad, Cara," Chrissy said, glancing up briefly. "You gave it your best shot."

"Yes, well..." Caroline said. "I guess I'll go take a shower. I take it you're going out with Hunter tonight?"

Chrissy looked up and beamed. "We're going out to celebrate. Hunter says he's so proud of me, he's taking

me to the Bois de Bologne." Chrissy said the name of
the restaurant slowly, trying to pronounce the unfamiliar
words with the same accent she'd heard Hunter use. "I
gather it's been featured in all the gourmet magazines. I
know I'm going to blow my diet, but I don't care. Now
that I'm a famous artist, it doesn't matter so much if I
turn into a blimp!" She giggled, then a thought struck
her. "Caroline, I've never been to such a fancy restaurant. Maybe you'd better give me a quick lesson on
which fork to use when."

"Just fake it, you'll be fine, you always are," Caroline said, and walked out of the room.

"Hey, what's eating you?" Chrissy called after her,
then shrugged and returned to her painting. Something
in the back of her mind nagged that she should go after
Caroline to find out why she was upset, but she brushed
aside the thought. *There's nothing I can do about it anyway*, she told herself. *I can't help her get the part, and if
this other girl really is more talented, then there's nothing
Cara can do. I'd only make things worse by being nosy.*

Caroline had gone out again by the time Chrissy finished painting, and she was still out when Hunter came
by for Chrissy at seven. She'd decided to borrow Caroline's black beaded sweater with the very low-cut back
to wear with the long red skirt she'd just bought.
Chrissy thought the result was very sophisticated. For a
second in front of the mirror, she remembered the image
of herself as a city girl that she had conjured up before
leaving home. Now the image had become a reality.

The evening at the restaurant was almost perfect.
Hunter looked extremely handsome in a navy-blue dou-
ble-breasted suit, and he was as charming and attentive

as always. The waiters treated them with respect, hovering about with their silver serving trays. After a week of dieting, every mouthful tasted especially heavenly to Chrissy. She was also relieved to find that the knives and forks were not as complicated as she'd dreaded. All she had to do was glance at the couple sitting at a nearby table to find out which utensil to use.

How about that? she marveled, smiling at the waiter as he whisked away her plate. *Plain old Chrissy Madden has turned into a famous artist and a smooth city girl in one easy lesson! What will they say about this back home? I bet they wouldn't recognize me!*

She felt so pleased with herself, she even managed to keep her cool when the waiter set fire to the Cherries Jubilee Hunter had ordered for their dessert. *A couple of weeks ago, I probably would have thrown my glass of water on the cherries to put out the fire,* Chrissy thought in amusement. *I bet that's what the kids at home would do!*

"Don't you think flambé dishes are fun?" Hunter asked her as the waiter scooped still-flaming portions onto their plates. "I always order one just to see the flames," he went on.

Chrissy smiled. "I like flames, too," she said, "I like fireworks on the Fourth of July and gazing into winter fires."

"I once set fire to the dining room carpet when I was a kid," Hunter said. "My parents were having one of their parties, and they had set up some chafing dishes on the buffet to keep the food warm. Well, I tipped one over—flame and everything!"

"Oh, no, what happened?" Chrissy asked in concern.

"Oh, not much. I just destroyed an antique buffet and half a room of Chinese carpet." Hunter laughed. "Other than that, everything was fine!"

"I don't believe you take anything seriously," Chrissy scolded.

"Of course I don't. What is there to take seriously? My motto is to only do the things I enjoy—why bother with things that worry you? Life's too short."

"Maybe you're right," Chrissy said thoughtfully. "What use is worrying?"

"None at all, and it gives you wrinkles before you're old," Hunter said.

The rest of the evening passed smoothly. They finished their meal and drove up to Telegraph Hill, where they could see the bay glistening in the moonlight then turn around and see the sparkling lights of the city.

"That was a wonderful evening," she whispered to Hunter as they finally pulled up in front of the Kirbys' apartment house. "I don't think I'll ever forget tonight."

Hunter laughed. "You make it sound as if we'll never have another chance to do this," he said. "All the restaurants in San Francisco aren't planning to close up, are they?"

"Of course not," Chrissy said lightly. "I just meant that it was a really special evening."

"Well, there are plenty more restaurants around here," Hunter said, "and I would love to take you to all of them. I love an excuse to eat!" He paused. "That reminds me—what do you think about having a celebration dinner for our committee? I mean, we did such a great job of organizing the art fair. None of the exhibits fell down on the judges, and there was enough food and drink for everyone. I think we were fantastic, don't you?"

"Fantastic," Chrissy agreed.

"So you think a dinner would be a good idea?"

"Oh, yes, sounds good to me," Chrissy agreed.

"Congratulations, then," Hunter said. "You've got the job."

"What do you mean?" Chrissy stammered.

Hunter laughed. "We'll have the dinner at my house and you can help cook it."

"Me?" Chrissy stammered. "You want me to cook a dinner for everyone? But I'm not even on the committee."

"That's okay," Hunter said. "It will be fun. We'll cook some really interesting things. Let's start thinking of a menu. Maybe we'll serve all flambé dishes!"

Chrissy remembered the rock-hard brownies she'd made at home, when the boys had used them for target practice. As she ran up the steps to the apartment a few minutes later, she thought, *I hope Caroline has some good recipes.* Then Chrissy recalled Caroline's odd behavior that afternoon, and hoped her cousin wouldn't mind helping her.

"I totally blew my diet last night," Chrissy said chattily as she ate her grapefruit on Sunday morning. "Hunter says that you should do the things you enjoy — and you know how I enjoy eating!"

Caroline only grunted.

"The food at Bois de Bologne is fabulous. Have you ever eaten there?" Chrissy went on. "We had Cherries

Jubliee for dessert. You know, they flambé them at the table. That alone must have been about a million calories."

Caroline poured herself a cup of coffee and walked over to the window.

"You want me to pour you some cereal?" Chrissy asked, watching Caroline sip her black coffee.

"No thanks," Caroline muttered. "I've got to go."

"Look, Cara," Chrissy said. "You need more than coffee for breakfast."

"You might. I'm fine," Caroline said, slamming her cup down on the counter.

"Are you mad at me?" Chrissy asked her cousin. "Have I done something?"

"No, nothing," Caroline mumbled.

"Then is there anything I can do to make you feel better?" Chrissy asked with concern.

"Just leave me alone," Caroline said, and walked from the room.

"We're all getting together today to finish painting the scenery for the ball," Chrissy called after her. "Do you think you can make it?"

"I doubt it," Caroline answered, not looking back.

"But you were so excited to be on the committee, Caroline," Chrissy said, following her down the hall.

"I can hardly not be at tryouts the day Madame selects the dancers for the opera, can I?" Caroline said frostily. "You never know, there might be a miracle and Tais might fall over and break her ankle!" She flung her gear into her ballet bag, her back turned to Chrissy, then left without saying another word.

Chrissy did not see her cousin again until late afternoon. She had spent a fun day helping paint romantic scenes of Venice. Hunter had been at his playful best, and the others in the group treated her differently now that she was a winning artist. Chrissy noticed that even Sacha spoke to her with a tinge of respect in her voice. It was strange and exciting to have them ask her opinion about the scenery they were designing for the ball. She found herself joining in an argument about the color of the Doges Palace, as if she had actually been to Venice.

To think I used to be scared of them, she thought as she painted bold strokes across a cardboard gondola. *Now that I know I'm just as good as they are, I can see that they aren't really scary at all. In fact, I think I'm finally fitting in to life in California. I hope this dinner we're having is as successful as the opening of the fair. It will have to be a really fancy dinner, I can see that. I'll impress them all, even Cara. I don't think she wants to admit that I've stopped being her hick cousin.*

Everyone was thrilled when Hunter told them about the dinner and announced that Chrissy would cook some of her specialties. *What specialties?* Chrissy thought.

"Make sure you do something with tofu, okay?" Rainbow said to her. "I'm a strict vegetarian, you know."

"And let's have lots of stuff without tofu," Dominic cut in. "Like veal parmagiana, maybe?"

Chrissy paid no attention to the persistent memory of her rock-hard brownies, and joined in the excited chatter. "All I know so far is that we're going to have something flambé," she said, giving Hunter a secret smile. When he winked at her in return, Chrissy's heart did a flip, ignoring the little voice in the back of her head that whispered, *Chrissy Madden, you are a first-class phony.*

Chapter 15

By the time Chrissy finally headed for home on Sunday, they had finished painting a whole wall to look like palaces along the Grand Canal in Venice. A paper and Styrofoam model of the Bridge of Sighs joined huge drawings of the palace and the ancient prison across one end of the auditorium.

Chrissy thought the auditorium looked wonderful— so dramatic, and *very* romantic. *I wonder how Venice, Italy, compares to our Venice?* she thought. *What's it like to ride in a real gondola beneath the Bridge of Sighs? Are there any fish in the canals?* Chrissy wanted to ask someone the answers to all the questions running through her mind, but she didn't dare. After all, she was supposed to be a world traveler too.

So Chrissy helped drag the cardboard gondolas to hide the front of the stage, and didn't say a word. When they were finished, she had to admit that it all looked very glamorous. *At least being here for the masked ball will be the next best thing to being in the real Venice*, she told herself. She couldn't wait to go to the ball with Hunter. He'd even promised to help her put together her costume from the collection of theatrical costumes his family kept in the attic.

Chrissy left the school auditorium feeling more confident than she had in weeks. The others accepted her as part of their group now, and she had the dinner and the masked ball to look forward to with Hunter. It was a beautiful clear afternoon, and as Chrissy tackled the hills on the way home, she felt like flying. She almost reached the top of the last hill when she saw Caroline walking ahead trudging upward as if her ballet bag was filled with lead.

"Cara, wait up," she called, running until she caught up to her cousin. "I've got so much to tell you," Chrissy said. "We had such a great time today. Mama mia— you should see the palazzos we painted. You'd think you were in St. Marks Square. And do you know what? Hunter thinks he has a couple of Pierrot costumes at home for us to wear to the ball. That would be *très chic* for the carnival in Venice, wouldn't it?"

Caroline stopped walking and leaned against a lamppost, dropping her ballet bag on the sidewalk.

"Cara, are you okay?" Chrissy asked. "Here, give me that bag." She reached over and picked it up.

"I don't know what's the matter with me, I feel so tired," Caroline said.

"Caroline, I knew something like this would happen," Chrissy said severely. "You've been starving yourself."

"And all for nothing, too," Caroline said, staring out

across the street. "She got the part today. Tais and Carl. They went off to practice together."

"I'm really sorry, Cara," Chrissy said. "I know how much you wanted that part, and I know how hard you tried."

"Well, it's all over now," Caroline said.

"Maybe it's all for the best," Chrissy comforted. "Now you can come back to your friends and help us get ready for the ball. The kids on the committee are so amusing, aren't they? We had this big argument about whether to paint all the gondolas black. I thought that they would look better painted dark blue and green. I mean, artistically they would look better. Even though they are black in Venice, this is a symbolic Venice, isn't it? I think I finally convinced them. But I'm sure you'll be a big help with the final touches and the costumes. Oh, and I'm going to need your advice for a dinner I'm cooking for the committee. Something flambé, we thought, and we have to have at least one tofu dish."

"You sound like you've certainly been getting along well with everyone," Caroline said.

"Oh, I have—I really feel part of the group now. Of course, they respect me as an artist, which is nice, but I really feel quite at home with them. In fact, I really feel that I can be just as witty as anyone there—except Hunter, maybe, but then Hunter is a true Renaissance man. Sacha was saying so this morning."

Caroline turned and looked at her cousin directly. Her eyes narrowed. "What's that you're wearing?" she asked.

Chrissy grinned. "It's your sweatshirt."

"Who said you could wear that?"

"But Cara, you always let me wear your things. You said yourself I've got nothing right to wear with Hunter."

Caroline stared at Chrissy, making her cousin feel uncomfortable. "But that's my favorite sweatshirt."

"I didn't think you'd mind," Chrissy said.

"And . . . and you've got paint on it, too!" Caroline stammered.

"Only a tiny blob. I know—I'm sorry about that. Hunter flicked it on me, but I'll get it off, don't worry."

"I can't believe this," Caroline said.

"It's no biggie," Chrissy replied, shrugging her shoulders. "A little drop of paint on a sweatshirt is not the end of the world." But Chrissy knew by the fierce look in Caroline's eyes that her cousin didn't agree.

"What a traitor you've turned out to be," Caroline began in a tight voice. "I felt sorry for you so I brought you along to *my* committee. I taught you what to say so you wouldn't sound like a freak, and I even lent you my clothes so that you wouldn't look like a freak, and what do you do in return? You take my place, you become everyone's darling, you start acting like a big shot, and you even steal my favorite clothes. You don't care two hoots about me really, so don't pretend you do!"

"Hey, Cara, that's not true and you know it!" Chrissy said, defending herself. People were looking at the girls as they passed them on the sidewalk, but for once Caroline didn't seem to care.

"Oh, no?" she went on even louder. "When I came home yesterday feeling depressed, you didn't even want to hear about it. You were too busy doing your wonderful painting and thinking you were the queen of the art world. Well, I've got news for you—the painting stunk."

"What do you know about it?" Chrissy began, her own voice rising to match her cousin's. "Your work didn't win the contest, did it? Maybe you're just jealous because things have been going so well for me. I've found my true place—a place where I belong among creative people, and you don't like that, do you? You'd rather I stayed your naive little country cousin so you could feel sorry for me."

"Correction, I'd rather you'd never come here," Caroline retorted. She grabbed her bag from Chrissy. "Now would you leave me alone? I'm sick of having someone one step behind me all my life." She hurried on ahead, and as Chrissy watched from behind, she staggered.

"Cara!" Chrissy screamed in horror, sprinting toward her cousin and catching her just before she fell. Propping Caroline's arm around her neck, she dragged her to a short flight of stairs outside a nearby house.

"Oh, Chrissy, I feel so strange," Caroline murmured. "Everything is swinging around." She leaned back against a step, her face white as a sheet.

"Sure it is. You're totally weak from not eating," Chrissy said, sitting next to her cousin on the step. "Just rest for a while, then I'll get you home."

Caroline closed her eyes. "I tried so hard, Chrissy," she said in a broken voice. "I wanted to dance in that opera so badly. I thought that if only I could get down to a hundred five pounds I'd float like Tais, and Carl would be able to lift me. . . ."

"But Cara," Chrissy said gently, "some things are

just not meant to be. You were not meant to be
hundred five pounds. You can't change the person you
are."

"You're right," Caroline said. "I guess if we weighed
the same, Tais would still be better. She's just a born
dancer and I'm not. I have to work really hard just to
be as good as I am."

"You're better than most people," Chrissy said
warmly. "You have a talent to be proud of."

"But it's not enough, Chrissy," Caroline said flatly. "I
want Carl. I want him to look at me as if he's never seen
such a graceful dancer. But now he looks at Tais instead."

Chrissy put her arm around Caroline's waist. "Come
on, let's go home," she said. "I'll fix you a good meal. I
need all the practice I can get."

Slowly Caroline got to her feet. "Chrissy, I'm sorry I
yelled at you. I wasn't mad at you. I was mad at me for
failing."

"Hey, what's all this talk about failing?" Chrissy
said, supporting her cousin as she took a hesitant step
forward. "Just because one part didn't work out for you
and one boy in the world didn't notice you—big deal!
You set yourself goals that were just too high this time.
Like me setting myself a goal to be an instant sophisticated person. I know I'm not really sophisticated, Cara.
I can pretend to be all I like, but only on the outside.
Inside I'm still plain old me."

Caroline turned and smiled. "I like the plain old you
better," she said. "The new Chrissy scared me."

"She scares me a bit, too," Chrissy admitted. "Sometimes I hear myself talking and I don't believe the words

hat are coming out of my mouth. It's as if I'm a robot
programmed to act a certain way."

"Then come back to your old self, Chrissy," Caroline
said.

"But what about Hunter?" Chrissy asked with a big
sigh. "He expects me to be the new, improved Chrissy."

"But I need you, too," Caroline said in a small voice.
"I need your plain old common sense. I should have
listened to you about the dieting. You kept on telling me
that I needed to eat more, and you were right. Next
time don't let me be so dumb, okay?"

Chrissy rolled her eyes. "You try telling Caroline
Kirby something she doesn't want to hear!" she said.
"You can be pretty stubborn for a sweet and gentle little
thing!"

Caroline leaned against Chrissy. "But don't give up
on me, Chrissy, okay? I know I set myself impossible
goals. I guess sometimes I want to be perfect. . . ."

"Who doesn't?" Chrissy asked with a chuckle.

"I do believe," Caroline began, "that I take life much
too seriously."

Chrissy nodded in agreement.

"You're a pretty neat cousin, you know that?" Caroline asked.

"Not nearly as neat as you, especially around the
house," Chrissy said.

"You know what I mean."

"Sure I know."

"And you understand how I feel sometimes. It's nice
to share things. . . ."

They both looked at Chrissy's sweatshirt. Chrissy's
face flushed. "Cara," she began, "about your shirt—"

"I said I was sorry for yelling," Caroline interrupted.

"No, I'm the one who should be sorry," Chrissy said firmly. "I had no right to take your clothes without asking. Besides, I ought to thank you for yelling at me."

"Huh?" Caroline asked. "What do you mean?"

"Well, my brothers and I always yell at each other," Chrissy replied. "So you made me feel right at home."

Chrissy looked at her cousin mischievously as a weak laugh escaped from Caroline's lips. Then they made their way slowly down the hill.

Chapter 16

"How do I look?" Chrissy asked a few nights later, as she swept into the living room where Caroline sat curled up in an armchair.

Caroline looked up, then her jaw dropped open. "Oh, wow!" she said.

"Do you like it?" Chrissy asked. "I got it in Chinatown today. I thought I needed something pretty impressive to wear to dinner at Hunter's house."

Chrissy turned around slowly to model the slim ankle-length skirt slit up past her knee on one side, and the bodice in brilliant red Chinese brocade. Chrissy's spiked heels, long red fingernails, and normally flyaway hair—now coiled around her head in a neat French braid—completed the look.

"Oh, wow," Caroline said again. "Chrissy, I would never have recognized you. I'd have walked right past you in the street, you look so different."

"You haven't said I look nice," Chrissy replied in a hurt tone. "I think I look spectacular."

"You do," Caroline said. "It's just that . . . well, you don't look like you! You look like a model or a movie star or something."

"Do you think Hunter will like it?" Chrissy asked, looking unsure at Caroline from behind a layer of makeup.

Caroline grinned. "I think his eyes will leap right out of his head. You'd better not let him catch you alone tonight, or watch out!"

"That good, huh?"

"Chrissy, I'd never have believed it," Caroline answered. "You certainly don't look like the same girl who arrived in San Francisco a couple of months ago. How did you put together an outfit like this?"

"I saw the dress when I was walking home the other day," Chrissy said, "and since our dinner is going to have a Chinese flavor, I thought it would be a neat idea." She paused to smooth the skirt. "I borrowed some money from your mother, and I'm going to ask my mom to send my birthday money early so I can pay her back. I've been dying to show you the dress, but I wanted to surprise you."

"You certainly have," Caroline said. "Now how on earth are you going to manage to cook, looking like that?"

"I have the recipe all ready," Chrissy said. "I'm just going to throw the stuff together—with your help, of course."

"What did you finally decide on?"

"Stuffed grape leaves for appetizers. Chinese salad with tofu for the vegetarians, and duck with lichee sauce for the meat eaters. Hunter can light the lichee sauce and we'll serve it flambé," Chrissy said, fidgeting nervously in her elegant clothes. "I spent hours looking through your mother's recipe books trying to find things that sounded hard but were really easy. I hope these are as easy as they look."

"Well, you just tell me what I can do to help," Caroline said, "and for heaven's sake, bring an apron."

"Don't worry, I know what I'm like when I'm let loose in the kitchen," Chrissy said, her bright red lips curving into a wide grin. "I do not intend to spoil my glamorous image by spilling lichee sauce on my dress. In fact, when I enter the room I aim to look marvelous." She raised her hand to brush away an imaginary wisp of hair. "Simply marvelous, dahling . . . Ow!"

"What's the matter?" Caroline asked.

"Dumb fingernail," Chrissy growled. "I scratched my eye with the dumb fingernail. I'm not used to nails this long."

Caroline started to laugh. "What a very unsophisticated thing to do," she said. "You'd better not let the others know."

"You'd better not tell them," Chrissy said, laughing as she tried to stop her eye from watering without touching her makeup. "I guess I'd better get my food packed to take over to Hunter's. He's coming at six-thirty." She started for the kitchen, then stopped and put her hand up to her face. "This stupid eye really hurts," she said. "I can't stop it watering."

Caroline got up. "Let me take a look."

"Watch my makeup," Chrissy warned nervously. "Try not to smudge my mascara."

"Forget the makeup," Caroline said. "Chrissy, you've

really scratched your eye badly. It looks horrible. I think you should see a doctor."

"But I haven't got the time."

"But you could go blind or something. There is a serious scratch on your eye, Chrissy. Don't you think you should do something about it?"

"I'm sure it will be okay, if I can just stop it from watering so much," Chrissy said. She went back to the kitchen and started taking out cans and jars. But after a few minutes she returned to the living room.

"It's no use, Caroline," she admitted. "It does really hurt, and it's streaming. I can't see anything."

"I'll get my dad," Caroline said. "He'll take you to the emergency room."

"But what about Hunter? I haven't got time—he'll be here in less than an hour."

"I'll call Hunter. Perhaps he won't mind dropping by to pick me up instead, so I can get things ready for you."

"That would be great, Cara, but what are you going to tell him? Don't tell him the truth, for heaven's sake. He'll laugh. They'll all laugh."

"Chrissy, if they're really your friends, they'll be worried about you."

"I don't know," Chrissy said hesitantly. "I really don't want them to know the truth. I mean, how dumb can you get—cutting your eye with a fake fingernail? Tell them . . . let's see . . . tell them I was painting and there was a sudden earthquake and my brush went in my eye."

Caroline had to laugh. "Chrissy, even in San Francisco we don't have earthquakes that only affect one house. You'd better think again."

"I can't think," Chrissy wailed. "My eye hurts and I'm getting scared."

"I'll get my dad," Caroline said again, and ran into the hallway. "And don't worry about telling the others. I'll think of something."

Two hours later Chrissy stood looking at herself in the emergency room mirror. One half of her face was covered with a big white pad, its whiteness creating a stark contrast to the vivid makeup on the other half of her face. The doctor had put drops in her eye, and it no longer hurt. In fact, she felt ready to go to the dinner party, except for her embarrassment over the huge bandage.

"You must keep your eye covered for two days, and then I want to see it again," the doctor said.

"You mean I have to wear this tonight? It looks terrible, and I'm going to a party," Chrissy pleaded.

The doctor frowned. "You must give the eye time to heal itself. That was a nasty scratch, you know. You don't fool around with eyes—you've only got two to last you a lifetime."

I hope they don't laugh when they see me, Chrissy thought. Caroline's voice echoed through her head: "If they're really your friends, they'll be worried about you." *Are they really my friends?* Chrissy wondered. *Is Hunter really my friend? Have we ever sat down together and talked about ourselves? We just see an image of each other—I like the image that I see, but I don't really know Hunter.*

"I don't look like myself at all," she said to the unfamiliar face in the mirror. Her mind drifted back to Sunday, when she had run into Caroline on the way home.

She saw herself talking to her cousin as Caroline leaned against the steps. She heard her own voice saying, "You can't be somebody you're not." Why hadn't she thought that this applied to her, too?

"This person isn't me," she said to the mirror. "And I want to be me again. But I'm in this mess too deep now to get out."

The nurse came in to lead her back to the waiting room. Caroline's father took one look at her and chuckled.

"That's most impressive," he said. "You look as if you're the victim of an exploding bomb, instead of the victim of an extra-long fake fingernail. How are you feeling?"

"Fine," Chrissy said. "I'm feeling just fine. The doctor put drops in my eye, and it doesn't hurt at all now. I feel like a big phony with this huge bandage on."

"Well, Chrissy, I think it's very becoming. If I didn't know better, I would have thought it was part of your glamorous outfit," her uncle joked. "Do you feel like going to your party or do you want me to drive you home?"

Chrissy hesitated. Half of her didn't want to go to the party anymore, but the other half didn't want Caroline and Hunter to feel she had let them down. "The party, I guess," she said at last. "I can't leave Caroline to do the cooking without me."

"Okay, the party it is," Uncle Richard replied warmly, and led her out of the hospital.

Chrissy gazed out of the car window a few minutes later with her one good eye, and tried to think of a story to tell the group at Hunter's house that would not make her sound like a complete klutz. She recalled something her uncle had said—that she looked like the victim of a bomb. What if there had been a bomb scare in a big department store and everyone had panicked and she'd been pushed against a counter in the rush? That sounded plausible, and certainly dramatic, but not klutzy—didn't it? She tossed the idea around her brain, perfecting her story until she had decided exactly what she was going to say.

In fact, she was feeling confident again by the time they turned onto Hunter's street. But when she caught her first glimpse of his house, all her confidence fled. She'd expected his house to be big and elegant, but she hadn't dreamed it would be anything like this. It reminded Chrissy of a red-brick English castle. It had a landscaped garden in front, and a huge wooden door studded with nails.

She was just opening her mouth to tell her uncle to keep driving when the front door opened and Hunter peered around it.

"Here she is now," he called, running out to open the car door for her. "You poor thing, Chrissy. What a terrible thing to happen," he said, taking her hand. "Come on in, we've got everything under control and we're all waiting for you."

He led her into a marble entrance hall lined with ferns and statues. Chrissy just had time to absorb the curved staircase and the huge chandelier before Hunter steered her into a living room that Chrissy thought must be at least half the size of a football field. Faces looked up at her from the sofas by a roaring fire.

"Hi, Chrissy! How are you feeling?" Dominic asked.

"You poor thing," Sacha said, patting the seat next to her. "Come and sit down."

"We were so worried about you," said Rainbow.

All the voices blended together, but Chrissy knew they were all sincere. Nobody was laughing as she had expected, Chrissy thought with a lump in her throat. She felt as if she might cry at any moment.

"You okay?" Caroline asked softly, coming to meet her. Chrissy nodded, and Caroline went on. "Your recipes were just excellent, so we had no trouble at all. Hunter is a great cook, by the way—you should see him stir frying in the wok!"

Chrissy didn't dare ask what a wok was—she only vaguely recalled seeing the word in Aunt Edith's cookbook. She looked from one person to another, fighting back the strange panic rising inside her.

"We were so upset when we heard," Rainbow said in a worried voice. "What a terrible thing to happen to you."

"How exactly did it happen?" Sacha asked.

"There was a bomb scare," Chrissy said. Her mouth was so tense that she could hardly get the words out. "Everybody started running, and I got pushed into a glass counter."

"A glass counter?"

"Yes, you know, where they have the jewelry."

"Jewelry? On a cable car?"

"In Neiman-Marcus. You know—the department store."

There was a pause.

"You got hurt in Neiman-Marcus?" someone asked.

"Yes. There was a bomb scare."

Another pause.

"Caroline said that you got pushed off a cable car."

Chrissy opened her mouth to explain. The tension in her head was so great that she felt as if she might explode at any moment. "Caroline didn't understand," she said. "You see, when I came home I was upset and I'd just gotten off the cable car, so she must have thought . . ."

Oh, what's the use? Chrissy asked herself. She took a deep breath. "Neither of those things is what happened at all," she said. "I cut my eye with one of these false fingernails. I was wearing false fingernails because I was trying to be somebody I'm not. I'm not a general's daughter and I've never been to Europe. I'm not even artistic. That tower of cans—I only built it to amuse myself. It isn't art, it's just something my brothers and I used to do back home on our farm in Iowa. I'm sorry I deceived you all . . . I didn't mean to. I just got stuck with pretending . . . I'm really sorry. . . ."

Tears were stinging in both her eyes, making the scratched eye hurt again and blurring her vision in her good eye. Chrissy glanced around the room at everyone staring at her, then turned and ran toward the door. Her high heels clattered on the marble floor. A tall, middle-aged woman appeared on the curved staircase and looked at Chrissy in surprise.

"Is something wrong?" she asked.

"No, everything's fine. I just have to leave, that's all. I've just remembered something. Lovely party . . ." Chrissy mumbled as she wrenched open the front door and ran out into the cold night air.

She ran down the hill, half stumbling as her awkward heels caught in the cracks on the sidewalk. She had no idea where she was going. She wasn't even sure exactly how to find her way back to the Kirbys'. She just knew that she had to get away fast. She had to get back to real life, to a place where she could be plain old Chrissy Madden again—a fun-loving country girl who didn't go to foreign movies or art shows, and didn't eat tofu and lichees, and didn't dress up in slinky clothes. Everything around her was a blur through her tears. She heard someone call out, but she kept on running. All she could think was that if she ran far enough, she would be safe and secure and home where she belonged. Vaguely, she was aware of footsteps behind her, then an arm grabbed her.

"Chrissy, wait up. Chrissy—how can you run so fast in such a tight skirt?" Hunter was panting as he held on to her arm.

Chrissy tried to pull herself free. "Let me go, please. I just want to go home. I feel so bad about everything . . . I'm so sorry, Hunter."

"You can't walk home from here," Hunter said. "It's too far. And besides, you can't walk home alone in the dark. I'll drive you if you really want to go."

"Of course I want to go," Chrissy said. "I don't belong here. I've made a fool of myself and I've made a fool of you. You must hate me."

"Of course I don't hate you, you crazy coot," Hunter said softly. He caressed her arm. "Chrissy, why didn't you tell me the truth earlier? Why did you let me go on thinking you were someone else?"

Chrissy let out a little sob. "I thought you wouldn't be interested in me if you found out who I really was," she said. "I thought you'd laugh at a girl from Iowa."

There was silence. "You are a dummy," Hunter said

at last. "Do you know what you've made me do, just for you? You've made me go to art shows and horrible concerts and movies I didn't understand. . . ."

Chrissy turned to look at him, not quite sure she'd heard correctly. He gazed down at her tenderly, his eyes crinkling in the corners.

"I did what?" she stammered.

"You made me go to concerts where people played garbage-can lids."

Chrissy's jaw dropped open. "But didn't you like all those concerts and things?" she asked.

"Let's put it this way," Hunter said, "I can think of better things to do with my time. I only took you to places like that because I thought that's what you liked. I thought that some creative genius from Europe would want a huge dose of culture."

"What do you really think of all this cultural stuff?"

"I'm not too thrilled about it," Hunter answered. "Of course, I have to put up with quite a bit, because of my parents. We live, breathe, and eat culture in my house, so I'm used to it. But if I had a choice, I'd go to a good rock concert anytime over garbage-can lids and vacuum cleaners."

Chrissy shook her head as if she couldn't believe what she was hearing. "So you only did those things to impress me?"

"Sure," Hunter said with a grin. "When I first saw you in the gym, you were making jokes about the bleachers. You tossed back your hair and laughed, and I thought to myself, That girl looks like a lot of fun. Then I came over to start up a conversation with you and I found that you'd built that sculpture, and I said to myself, 'Hunter, a girl like this will expect you to be serious and arty,' so I switched on my arty personality —the one I have to use when I'm with my parents at the symphony. And you fell for it, so I had to keep it up."

Chrissy started to laugh. "I don't believe this," she said. "You were trying to impress me?"

"You bet," Hunter said. "I didn't want you to say, 'Get lost, you uncultured creep!'"

"Oh, Hunter," Chrissy said, gazing up at him, "if you knew how much time and energy I put into being the sort of person you thought I was. Caroline even gave me lessons on art and music and world travel. And the whole time I had to be careful of what I said in case I slipped up."

Hunter slid his arms around her waist. His hands were very warm through the thin silk of her dress. "You know what?" he asked.

"No. What?"

"We've wasted a lot of time," he said. Then he drew her toward him and kissed her right there on the windy street corner while a cable car clanged its way past.

Chapter 17

Chrissy opened the piece of paper for the fifth time and looked down at the familiar large scrawl. How could one piece of paper make you feel so bad? she wondered. There wasn't much real news on it, but just the feeling it conveyed was enough to upset all of Chrissy's plans.

"Hi, Chrissy," she read again. It was funny to be able to read with both eyes, now that the patch had been removed, Chrissy thought. She continued reading.

Sorry I haven't written lately, but you know what I'm like with writing. It's bad enough to get my English assignments done for school this year. Why do teachers think that guys like me need to know about crazy German writers who died a hundred years ago? We've just read a story about a man who changed into a cockroach! Does that sound like something that will be useful when I'm driving a tractor?

Anyway, enough boring stuff, or my hand will give up before I've said what I want to say. I only wanted to say that I miss you, Chrissy. Your letters have stopped sounding homesick, so I'm a little (no, make that a lot) worried that maybe you are beginning to like it there better than here. I hope not. I'm counting the days until you come home again. Do you know what I did? I made myself a big calendar from now until next June and I'm crossing off each day before I go to bed at night. I can't wait until the crosses are more than the blank days—does it sound like I've finally flipped? I hope not, because you won't want to come back to a guy who is loony tunes.

Nothing's much fun without you around, Chrissy. Halloween is coming up and I keep remembering how we took the little kids around last year and pretended we were only doing it for them, when we had a better time than they did. Do you remember that house I crawled up to on my knees so they thought I was only a kindergartener? I got a lot of candy there! Anyway, I've decided I'm too old for that stuff this year. Harry Daniels is having his usual party, so I guess I'll go along to that.

The football team is doing great, but without me. I chipped a bone in my foot during practice and now I'm out for the rest of the season. Bummer, huh? I was really mad that it was during practice. It wouldn't be so bad if I'd hurt my foot to help us win a game. Chip Wilson stepped on my foot—that's how it happened. Don't laugh, okay? So I'm sitting on the bench all alone during the games, thinking about you. None of the cheerleaders jump around as much as you do—and none of them can yell as loud. Don't come back as a sophisticated city girl who doesn't yell and jump around, okay? I get scared sometimes that I won't know you when you come back.

And don't faint, but I've decided I might go to college after all. I mean, if you are planning to go, I sure couldn't be away from you for four whole years. Two months have been bad enough.

Must go now. My dad's yelling something about slopping the hogs.

Love, Ben

"Chrissy? Are you home?"

"In here, Caroline," Chrissy shouted back from the bedroom.

Caroline opened the door to find the room neat and uncluttered, and Chrissy curled on her bed. "Mama mia," Caroline said. "Are you sick or something?"

"Me? No, why?" Chrissy asked.

"Because it's only four hours before the masked ball, and I expected to come home from ballet and find you in the middle of a mountain of stuff, getting ready."

Chrissy looked up. "I don't feel like getting ready yet," she said.

"But you always get ready days before," Caroline pointed out. "You were already trying on nail polish yesterday. Is something wrong?"

"Not really," Chrissy said. "I'm just having second thoughts about this dance, that's all."

"But Chrissy, everything is straightened out. All the kids know the truth about you and they all understand why you acted the way you did. Hunter said he likes you just the way you are, so what have you got to worry about?"

Chrissy shrugged her shoulders.

"And besides," Caroline went on, "I'm sure you'll have fun tonight. Rock music, dancing, food—all the things you like best, and fun people, too. I personally can't wait."

"You're going with Alex, then?" Chrissy asked.

Caroline looked amazed. "Who else would I go with?"

"I just got the impression you were getting tired of Alex."

"I don't know what made you think that. I still like Alex as much as I ever did."

"Maybe it was all the fuss over a guy named Carl?" Chrissy asked innocently.

Caroline's cheeks flushed and she looked down. "That was just crazy," she said. "I don't know what was the matter with me, acting like that over a total stranger."

"But you said he gave you goose bumps."

Caroline smiled. "He did, but then so do certain movie stars, and I really wouldn't want to date them. Goose bumps aren't as important as the boy being a nice person."

"So Carl didn't turn out to be such a nice person?" Chrissy asked. "Or didn't you ever find out."

Caroline sank onto her bed. "I was talking to Tais this morning," she said.

"Tais—I thought you wanted to attack her with my chisel?"

"That was before I'd ever talked to her. She fell and hurt her ankle this morning, and I helped her wrap it up. It's funny that I wished something like that would happen to her last week," Caroline said, but today I was glad she hadn't hurt herself too badly. I never really knew her before. She told me all about Carl."

"What about him?" Chrissy asked curiously.

"You know I thought he was shy because he didn't mix much?" Chrissy nodded. "Tais says he's not shy at all. He just thinks so much of himself that he won't bother with ordinary dancers. He told her he was so glad that I didn't get picked to dance with him, because he could tell at a glance that I wasn't professional enough for him."

"What a nerve!" Chrissy said.

"Tais says he only wants to talk about himself, and he really objects to sharing a duet with her. She said he'd lift himself up if he could! She was really funny, but she made me see how far I've got to go before I'm a *real* dancer. Remember how I said it all seemed to come so easily to her? Not true at all, Chrissy. That girl lives, breathes, and sleeps dance." Caroline stretched her legs out and pointed her toes. Then, still pointing her toes, she lifted her legs until they were perpendicular to her body. "She gets up at six to put in an hour's practice before school," she continued. "Her folks have built her a complete practice room at home and she works there every morning and every night, as well as in all her classes." Caroline dropped her legs on the bed. "No wonder she's good. She deserves it. It made me realize that I'll probably never be that dedicated."

"You'll just have more fun," Chrissy said. "I'm glad you didn't ditch Alex. He's so nice, and I think he's so right for you."

"I know," Caroline said. "It's just that sometimes I get scared that I might be stuck with him for the rest of high school. I don't mean that I don't like having him around—I really do—but I want lots of boyfriends before I'm grown up. I want to know for sure which man is right for me, because when I get married, I want it to be for keeps."

"I feel the same way," Chrissy said, "which is one of the reasons I'm scared about going to the dance to-night."

"Why, do you think Hunter will want to elope with you?" Caroline joked.

Chrissy laughed. "That I can't imagine," she said. "No, it's this." She brought out the letter from under her pillow.

"From Ben?" Caroline asked.

Chrissy nodded. "It came this morning," she said. "It was such a sweet letter, Caroline, and he's missing me so much. He said he's made himself a huge calendar for his wall and he crosses off every day that passes until I get home. And if I go to college, he says he'll go, too, because he couldn't stand four years without me."

"Wow, that sounds serious," Caroline said.

"I know." Chrissy sighed. "I can't plan my future so many years ahead. How do I know what sort of person I'll be then? I might even choose to go to concerts with vacuum cleaners and create hundreds of towers of soda cans for every art gallery in the world!"

Caroline looked up, horrified, and Chrissy laughed at her cousin's expression. "Don't worry," she said. "I do know that I'm no artist! Your mother's paintings—now that's really art. There is no way I could paint pictures like that if I lived to be a hundred."

"If you took some serious classes, maybe," Caroline suggested, but Chrissy shook her head.

"I don't have any talent. I knew that in the back of my mind all along. No—the green horse will be the last record of my artistic career, and all that's good for is a game of pin the tail on the donkey!"

Caroline laughed, too. "Oh, Chrissy, I am glad you're back to your old self," she said. "I was beginning to worry that you were becoming a real culture vulture."

"Not me," Chrissy said. "I couldn't have held out much longer. I would have started laughing in the wrong places during my next foreign film."

"So what are you going to do about Hunter? You still like him, don't you?"

Chrissy nodded. "That's just the problem," she said. "I do still like him. He makes me laugh and he also gives me goose bumps. But I don't know what to do about Ben."

"You mean you feel guilty?"

Chrissy nodded again. "You see, I know that Hunter isn't really right for me. Even if he doesn't really like all that high brow stuff, he's still from such a different background. Look at his house—servants and statues, and mixing with famous people—he lives in another world, and I know I could never be part of it."

"So what are you going to do? Break up with him?"

"I wish I knew," Chrissy said. "The trouble is that I don't want to. Who would walk out on Prince Charming before midnight?" She turned over and lay on her back, staring at the ceiling. "I wish I knew what I wanted," she said. "I want to have a good time while I'm here, but I don't want to get too involved with a guy, and I don't want to hurt Ben."

"So talk to Hunter about it."

"I'll try," Chrissy said. "I get the feeling that Hunter isn't into serious conversations. He'd make a joke about it, and I'd never really know what he was feeling. That's just the problem, Cara. I don't know the person underneath at all, but I like what's on the surface. I'm so confused. Tell me what to do."

Caroline sighed. "I can't do that, Chrissy. It's your life. Only you know what you want out of it. If you really care about Ben, then I guess you shouldn't get too involved with Hunter. But if you only feel guilty about Ben because you feel obligated to stick with him, then maybe it's time to break free."

"I don't know Cara," Chrissy said. "I just don't know."

Chapter 18

"Are you having fun?" Alex asked Chrissy that night as he and Caroline rested on the sidelines during a pause in the dancing.

Chrissy nodded. "This is the first time we've stopped dancing all evening. Hunter is complaining that he'll be worn out by the time he's eighteen if I don't slow down. He's gone to get us some punch."

She took off her mask and fanned herself with it.

"I must say you both look terrific," Alex went on. "Those Pierrot clown costumes are really from the Carnival in Venice, aren't they?"

Chrissy nodded. "They came from Hunter's family. Do you know he has a whole attic full of costumes? We could have been anything from a gorilla to a prince and princess."

"The gorilla might have been fun," Alex said.

"That's what Hunter said, too," Chrissy remarked with a smile. "He said he'd be able to grab strange girls and they'd never know who he was. But he decided it would be too warm in the furry costume."

Caroline turned to her cousin. "Are you glad you came to the ball?" she asked in a low voice as the music started up again. "Are you any clearer about things?"

"Not at all," Chrissy said, then grinned. "But I decided—aw, what the heck, I'm not going to spoil a good party by moping around. My dad always says that things have a habit of sorting themselves out if you leave them alone. Tonight I intend to eat, drink, and be merry!"

Then she spotted Hunter and darted off to help him with the drinks.

"Let's take them out onto the terrace," Hunter suggested. "It's getting too warm in here."

"Aren't you glad you didn't wear your gorilla suit now?" Chrissy teased as they pushed open the doors and walked out into the clear, cool night.

"You bet," Hunter agreed. "I just realized that I'd be missing a lot with my lips trapped behind a gorilla face." He leaned across and brushed Chrissy's lips with his. "That was just the appetizer," he whispered. "You wait for the main course." He took the glass from her hand and set it down on a stone ledge. Then he drew her toward him. The kiss this time was not a light brush, but intense and demanding.

"Hunter," she stammered when he released her at last. "We're at a school dance. What if the principal comes out?"

Hunter laughed. "We'll show him kissing for advanced students," he said. "But you're right. It is kind of crowded here." He ran his finger along her arm.

"Chrissy, I've got a little idea. Why don't we go for a drive?"

"But the dance isn't over yet," Chrissy said, confused.

"Aren't you getting a little tired of dancing? I know I am," Hunter said. "Let's take a drive along the bay. It will be beautiful this time of night. What do you say?"

"I don't know, Hunter," Chrissy said hesitantly.

"You're right," Hunter said. "It is too cramped in that little Porsche. I have an even better idea. This friend of mine has a houseboat in Sausalito. He's in movies and he's never in town. The houseboat is just sitting there, and he said I could use it anytime. Doesn't that sound great?"

Chrissy swallowed hard. "Look, Hunter," she began, then continued quickly, before she could change her mind. "There are a couple of things I think we should talk about. You see, I've got this boyfriend back home. I'm not sure how I feel about him, but I'm not ready for another commitment yet. I really like you, and I love being with you, but I don't want you to get any ideas . . . about us, I mean. Not long-term ideas."

To her horror Hunter threw back his head and laughed loudly. "Oh, Chrissy," he said, "you don't know me very well, do you? My longest commitment so far has been about one month. I'm just not a committed type of person. I get bored too easily, so you have nothing to worry in that direction. I promise you I won't be hanging around by Thanksgiving!"

Chrissy opened her mouth, then closed it again before she spoke. "But Hunter, what about those things you said the night of the dinner party? And you just suggested driving to a houseboat in Sausalito. I'm sure you weren't just planning to look at the view!"

Hunter stopped laughing and looked at her seriously. "So what are you trying to say?"

"Well, going alone with a guy to a houseboat . . . that sounds like pretty much of a commitment to me. . . ." Chrissy stammered.

Hunter looked amused again. "Chrissy, this is the 1980's, not the 1890's."

Chrissy took a deep breath. "Back where I come from a guy wouldn't suggest a thing like that unless he was pretty serious about a girl."

"Oh, yes, I'd forgotten about the backwoods of Iowa," he said easily. "I guess back there you still have your father along with the shotgun when you go courting, and you have to get married if someone sees you kissing in public." He started to laugh again.

Chrissy looked at Hunter's face. Suddenly his smiling eyes didn't look so enchanting anymore. "If you're trying to say we still have real values back home, then I guess you're right," she said.

"We have values here, too," Hunter said, "only they're more up to date. A girl from San Francisco wouldn't think twice about going to a houseboat with a guy she liked. You should learn what the real world's like, honeybunch."

"I already know what the real world is like," Chrissy said proudly. "But it's obviously different from yours, and I think it's a lot better. I wouldn't change a thing about it. I had a great time with you, Hunter, but I think I knew all along that we didn't belong together.

Now I'm going to head for home, so I guess you'll have to go to the houseboat alone."

For a second Hunter looked angry, then he laughed. "You're a neat kid, Chrissy," he said. "You're going to give some poor farmer a heck of a time one day!" He pulled her toward him before she could protest, and kissed her full on the lips before releasing her again. "Pity about the houseboat," he said. "I could have taught you a lot!"

Chrissy started to walk away, then turned and looked at him. "You might have found there isn't much I don't already know," she said, giving him a big smile. Then she ran back into the auditorium.

"Hey, Chrissy, where are you going? Where's Hunter?" Caroline asked, grabbing her as she ran past.

"I think I'm going to go on home," she said. "I've danced enough to last a lifetime."

"Did you and Hunter have a fight?" Caroline asked.

"Not really a fight. Let's just say that my dad was right. Things did sort themselves out. I found out that Hunter and I live on different planets."

"What happened?"

"He suggested going with him to a houseboat in Sausalito. Then he told me I was years behind the times because I didn't agree with him." Chrissy managed to smile.

Caroline laid her hand on Chrissy's arm. "I was afraid this would happen."

"Don't worry about it," Chrissy said. "It made things much easier. I finally admitted to myself that big brown eyes and great kissing are not the only things I want in life."

"They're not?" Alex asked with a grin.

Chrissy managed to laugh. "It's a good thing I managed to sort things out here and I didn't have to fight him off later. I don't think it would have been such a friendly parting if I'd given him a black eye!"

Caroline slipped her arm through Chrissy's. "Chrissy, I always said you were tough, and you are. Lots of people would have packed their bags and gone straight back to Iowa after what you've been through in the past few days."

"Not me," Chrissy said. "I have a very important mission here. Who else would make your life miserable if I weren't around?"

"You mean interesting, Chrissy," Caroline said. "I'm lucky to have you around to prevent my life from getting boring."

"Hey, I resent that," Alex said.

"You are lucky to have Alex, too," Chrissy pointed out. "I think you're terrific, Alex. If Caroline ever gets tired of you, remember I'm next in line."

"Over my dead body," Caroline said, laughing. She slipped her arm through Alex's, too. "I don't intend to get tired of him for a long, long time."

"I've got a great idea," Alex suggested. "What do you say we all go out and get some ice cream?"

Chrissy and Caroline both started to shake their heads to turn down Alex's invitation, then Chrissy laughed. "I just realized," she yelled. "Neither of us needs to be on a diet anymore! Let's go celebrate with the biggest sundaes ever!"

Arm in arm the three of them pushed their way across the crowded dance floor into the crisp San Francisco night.

Chapter 19

The next morning Chrissy sat on the window seat and looked out over the bay. It was early morning, and for once the city was completely quiet. No horns blared, no cable cars clanged, no sirens wailed. Across the room Caroline's even breathing was the only sound.

As peaceful as Sunday mornings back home, Chrissy thought.

She looked down at the blank sheet of paper in front of her.

"Dear Ben," she began hesitantly. "So much has been happening here, it's hard to know where to start." *And what to tell you that won't hurt you,* she thought with a frown. *I can't tell you, Ben, about Hunter and how crazy I acted. You'd think I was the world's biggest dummy. You wouldn't understand how flattered I was and how exciting it was for me to be part of his life for a while. But that's out of my system now. I know now that*

I never want to be a sophisticated lady—or an artist, for that matter.

I've been going to concerts and entering art shows. I won't go into all the details of the art show. You'd think the whole thing was crazy, and I guess it was. They gave prizes to the weirdest, ugliest things, and didn't look twice at the pretty ones. I still think that art should be beautiful, don't you? I guess people here would laugh at the pictures we have up on the walls at home. They'd call them old-fashioned and primitive, but I still like them. So you don't have to worry about me, Ben. I know now that being here won't change the real me. I'll still be the same Chrissy Madden you knew before. I'll still think the same things are important and the same things are beautiful. I guess I was born with good old farm horse sense and it would take a lot to shake that out of me.

And I miss you, Ben. You may not know about art and composers and foreign cities, but you're still pretty special to me. Keep crossing off those days. I'm hoping I'll be able to come home for Christmas—you might put in a good word for me with Mom and Dad next time you drop by for your cornbread. Don't get me wrong—I'm not dying of homesickness anymore. In fact, I'm having a great time and doing so many fun things, but nothing can make up for being far away from my family and friends. I really like Caroline—she's become like a sister to me—but I miss scrapping with those bratty brothers, and I sure miss watching an old red truck drive up to the house every evening. Is the truck still running okay? I can't wait to take a long ride in it the minute I get back!

Take care of yourself, Ben. I wish I were there to keep you company on the bench during football games.

Love always,
Chrissy.

Here's a sneak preview from *The Last Dance*, book number three of SUGAR & SPICE:

"You could enjoy life if you decided to," Alex said. "You have to stop putting so much pressure on yourself."

"How can I?" Caroline asked miserably. "My whole future is at stake here. I've reached the stage when I find out if I can really be a professional dancer or not. My teacher and my parents expect so much of me, and I'm not sure I'm ready—I'm not sure if I'll ever be ready. That's what's making me so tense."

Alex squeezed her arm gently. "Have you ever stopped to ask yourself what you really want for *you*?" he asked. "Do *you* really want all this pressure?"

"Of course not," Caroline snapped. "Who would want to live feeling that their head is about to explode every day?"

"Then don't live like it," Alex said. "Decide what

you really want. If you don't want to enter this competition, then don't."

"You don't know what you're talking about," Caroline said, wriggling clear of him and getting to her feet. "I have to enter it and what's more, I have to win it."

"Says who?" Alex demanded. "Other people or you?"

"Everybody!" Caroline shouted. "Everybody, including me."

"I don't," Alex said quietly. "I say you should enjoy life first and work for your goals second. I also say that if your goal doesn't make you happy, then maybe it's the wrong goal."

"Well, you wouldn't know, would you, because you don't have any real goals," Caroline said icily.

Alex got to his feet and looked Caroline in the eye. "How would you know, Caroline?" he asked quietly. "One hundred percent of your time is wrapped up in you. I was willing to take second place to you because I could see you needed all the support you could get, but I'm not willing to wait around forever. Just remember that. I'm a person, too, Caroline. I have feelings of my own." He turned, walked to the front door, and shut it behind him.

Caroline stood staring down the empty hallway as if she were made of stone. She found that she was shivering, even though the apartment was warm. In the several wonderful months they had been dating, she and Alex had never had a real fight. Sure, they'd disagreed a few times, and even had a major misunderstanding, but never like this—a real attempt to hurt each other with words. Somehow it was even more terrible that

Alex hadn't lost his cool. He hadn't raised his voice once, and hadn't stormed out. She was the one who had blown up, and the worst thing of all was that Alex had been totally right. She had never thought of his feelings. He was always Alex, who would be there to give her support when she needed it most. She didn't know what his dreams were. She didn't even go to cheer at his soccer games.

I deserve to lose him, she thought, feeling the great weight of despair settle on her. *I've been so wrapped up in my own problems that I haven't had time to think of anyone else. Surely Alex understands that. I must talk to him in the morning and make him understand that I really do love him and that I'll make time for him . . . if I can just get through this horrible contest first. . . .*

As she undressed, Caroline remembered her math homework, which she hadn't even started. *Oh well,* she thought, *I suppose I'll have to get up extra early tomorrow.* She climbed into bed, curling into a tight little ball and pulling her comforter over her head to shut out the world. Alex's words continued to nag her. What did she really want? Did she really want to win the contest and be a professional ballerina?

I wish I knew, she murmured over and over. *I wish I knew what I really wanted.*

One thing was certain, though: She definitely wanted Alex. *Why did I say such terrible things to him?* she asked herself. *I really hurt his feelings badly, and I didn't mean to. If only I can make it all right again tomorrow. . . .*

"Oh, Alex," she whispered into her pillow. "What would I do without you?"

ABOUT THE AUTHOR

Janet Quin-Harkin is the author of more than thirty books for young adults, including the best-selling *Ten-Boy Summer* and *On Our Own*, its sequel series. Ms. Quin-Harkin lives just outside of San Francisco with her husband, three teenage daughters, and one son.